Samuel French Acting Edition

Lady Precious Stream

by S. I. Hsiung

I0589040

‖ SAMUEL FRENCH ‖

SAMUELFRENCH.COM   SAMUELFRENCH.CO.UK

ISBN 978-0-573-61139-1

www.SamuelFrench.com
www.SamuelFrench.co.uk

FOR PRODUCTION ENQUIRIES

UNITED STATES AND CANADA
Info@SamuelFrench.com
1-866-598-8449

UNITED KINGDOM AND EUROPE
Plays@SamuelFrench.co.uk
020-7255-4302

Each title is subject to availability from Samuel French, depending upon country of performance. Please be aware that *LADY PRECIOUS STREAM* may not be licensed by Samuel French in your territory. Professional and amateur producers should contact the nearest Samuel French office or licensing partner to verify availability.

MUSIC USE NOTE

Licensees are solely responsible for obtaining formal written permission from copyright owners to use copyrighted music in the performance of this play and are strongly cautioned to do so. If no such permission is obtained by the licensee, then the licensee must use only original music that the licensee owns and controls. Licensees are solely responsible and liable for all music clearances and shall indemnify the copyright owners of the play(s) and their licensing agent, Samuel French, against any costs, expenses, losses and liabilities arising from the use of music by licensees. Please contact the appropriate music licensing authority in your territory for the rights to any incidental music.

IMPORTANT BILLING AND CREDIT REQUIREMENTS

If you have obtained performance rights to this title, please refer to your licensing agreement for important billing and credit requirements.

LADY PRECIOUS STREAM

STORY OF THE PLAY

This exotic play tells the romantic success story of a young Chinese maiden of noble birth who, as subsequent events prove, loved a humble gardener wisely and too well. Lady Precious Stream is the third daughter of His Excellency Wang Yun, the Prime Minister. Since his daughter has reached the maritally ripe old age of sixteen, the Prime Minister is determined to choose a son-in-law from the nobility and get his third and last daughter married. But Lady Precious Stream, with a mind and will of her own, has taken matters into her own dainty hands and, in a modest Chinese way, has quite a fancy for the humble Hsieh Ping-Kuei—her father's gardener, who can also furnish a verse when the occasion demands it. By the simple expedient of removing "an act of God," the tossing of an embroidered ball among the eligible suitors to determine the bridegroom, out of Divine hands, the royal maiden gets her gardener, and she is promptly ignored by her rich, regal relatives. She goes to live with her husband in an unpretentious cave, vowing never to return to her father's house unless she can do so as a lady of wealth.

The play then shows how, after eighteen hard years, the "tables are turned" for our heroine. Hsieh Ping-Kuei becomes a king; Lady Precious Stream sits as his queen in judgment on her harsh relatives. The good are rewarded, the bad are punished, and the audience is pleased and satisfied.

Copy of program of the first performance of "LADY
PRECIOUS STREAM," as produced at the Booth Theatre,
New York:

MORRIS GEST

Presents

LADY PRECIOUS STREAM

A Play in Four Acts
BY
S. I. HSIUNG
Staged by the Author
Settings by Watson Barratt

CAST
(In the order of their appearance)

HONORABLE READER .... *Mai-Mai Sze*

PROPERTY MEN .... { *Norman Stuart*
                               { *Jesse Wynne*

HIS EXCELLENCY WANG YUN, *the Prime Minister*
                                —*Clarence Derwent*

MADAM WANG, *his wife*.............*Molly Pearson*

SU, *the Dragon General, their eldest son-in-law*
                                —*Henry Morrell*

WEI, *the Tiger General, their second son-in-law*
                                —*Detmar Poppen*

GOLDEN STREAM, *their eldest daughter*...*Helen Kimm*

SILVER STREAM, *their second daughter*.*Marcella Abels*

PRECIOUS STREAM, *their third daughter*
                                —*Helen Chandler*

HER MAID .... *Sally Fitzpatrick*

HSIEH PING-KUEI, *the gardener*...*Bramwell Fletcher*

SUITORS .... { *Preston Tuttle, Will Claire,*
                              { *Harry Selby, Slater Barkentin*

THE PRINCESS OF THE WESTERN REGIONS
—*Natalie Schafer*

MA TA } ...*Her aides de camp*... { *Albert Whitley*
KIANG HAI } { *Preston Tuttle*

MAIDS TO THE PRINCESS { *Joan Adrian, Lilian Dushell,*
{ *Joan Miller, Sally Fitzpatrick*

GENERAL MU ....*Henry Morell*
EXECUTIONER .... *Gilbert Ralston*
THE MINISTER OF FOREIGN AFFAIRS......*Will Claire*
    CHINESE ATTENDANTS, WESTERN ATTENDANTS,
        SOLDIERS, CHINESE MAIDS, *etc.*

SCENES

ACT ONE

PART I—
    The Garden of the Prime Minister.
    On a New Year's Day.
PART II—
    The same. The Second of February.

ACT TWO

PART I—
    The Cave of Hsieh Ping-Kuei.
    One month later.
PART II—
    The same. Nine months later.

INTERMISSION TEN MINUTES

ACT THREE

PART I—
    The Western Regions. Eighteen years later.
PART II—
    The Cave. A short time later.

ACT FOUR

PART I—
> The Garden of the Prime Minister.
> The next morning.

PART II—
> The Temporary Court of the King of the Western Regions. The next day.

Lady Precious Stream

ACT ONE

SCENE I

SCENE: *See design.*
    Stage LIGHTS set on dim marks. House LIGHTS out. Blue FOOTLIGHTS on.
    When house LIGHTS out: GONG #1. READER enters between curtains to in front of curtain. SPOT on READER.

READER. *(To audience)* Good evening (afternoon), Ladies and Gentlemen. You are now introduced to the traditional Chinese stage, which, according to our humble convention, is not in the least realistic. Scenery is a thing we have never heard of, and the property men who are supposed to be unseen by the audience are taking an active part in the performance. The success or failure of a production is sometimes in their hands. They provide chairs for the actors to sit on and the cushions to kneel upon; and the case when the hero is to die an heroic death he can fall down majestically and without any hesitation, for the never-failing hands of the property men are always on the watch and will promptly catch him before any disaster can take place. Nevertheless they sometimes, in an excess of zeal, overdo their duty by even looking after the worldly com-

9

forts of the players. When the actor has just finished some long lines, they would present him a cup
of tea to ease the throat. These actions would certainly be condemned by a western audience but we
accept or rather pretend not to see them. There is,
at least, one advantage: if some accident happens to
the actor or property they can come forward and
put it right before the audience can decide whether
it is part of the play or not. (GONG #2. Curtain
up.) Now let us imagine that this unfurnished stage
represents the scene of the picturesque garden of
the Prime Minister, Wang Yun, who appears wearing a long black beard which indicates that he is not
the villain of the piece. In spite of his very long
beard, His Excellency is a middle-aged man who has
always found life easy and happy. As he is a man
of peppery temper he is sometimes cross when he
has really nothing to find fault with. He is a strict
master of his home, which he rules with an iron
hand, though his wife says that he should have
someone at his elbow. In Goverment he finds that
to rule a nation is much easier than to rule a family.
That is, no doubt, why we have so many prominent
statesmen in history. Madam, his wife, is a kind
lady of uncertain age. To her children she seems to
be more than a hundred, while to her husband she
is but a mere child. She is one of the women who
know the importance of the ancient female virtues.
To obey your father when young, to obey your husband when married, and to obey your children when
a mother. By obeying people all her life she has
acquired a benign look and a soft voice. Their eldest
son-in-law, Su, the Dragon General, is a famous
warrior because he always wins the battle when the
enemy's General knows less about making war than
he does. He knows nothing but enough to be aware
of his own ignorance. Their second son-in-law, Wei,
the Tiger General, is also a famous warrior because

he always has the best of luck though it would be impossible to find a worse soldier. He knows nothing and does less, but he talks endlessly and has consequently become famous. As for the daughters of the family, they are such charming young ladies that the author finds his English inadequate to describe their charms. However, charming ladies need no introduction—but we must warn you against Lady Precious Stream, our heroine, because she could make you put the halter willingly around your neck—if she chose to lead you along with her. The hero of the piece, Hsieh Ping-Kuei, gardener to His Excellency, is a man of deeds rather than words. So it would not do him justice if we vainly try to describe his merits, which, we hope, will prevent him from putting that halter willingly around his own neck. (READER *bows and exits down* L.)

ACT ONE

SCENE II

GONG #3. Stage LIGHTS up.

PROPERTY MEN *enter* L. *and* R. *and bow to audience—sit at their places.*

GONG #4. MUSIC.

Enter 1ST *and* 2D ATTENDANTS *from up* R. *They go downstage* R. 1ST ATTENDANT *crosses front of stage to down* L. 2D ATTENDANT *stays down* R.

WANG *follows* ATTENDANTS *on, going down* C. *Bows to audience.*

PROPERTY MAN L. *brings on table and places it down* L.

As WANG *starts to speak MUSIC stops.*

WANG. I am your humble servant, Wang Yun, the Prime Minister of the Emperor's Court. My consort's name is Chen. Although we have been happily married for twenty years, we are still childless. It is true that we have three daughters but that doesn't count; as you know, daughters leave their parents and become other people's property. My eldest daughter is called Golden Stream, who married Su, the Dragon General; the second is called Silver Stream, who married Wei, the Tiger General. The one dearest to my heart is the youngest, called Precious Stream—(PROPERTY MAN R. *places armchair* C.)—who will be sixteen next February. I have a mind to choose for her amongst the rich and young nobles for a son-in-law, but the little minx is as wilful as she is pretty, and refuses to obey my wishes. (ATTENDANTS *come to* C. *Pantomime opening large double door. They return to down* L. *and down* R. WANG *enters garden, stepping over threshold, and sits* C.) However, today's New Year's day; I will spread a feast here in my garden and have all my family present, and let my wife, my two sons-in-law and my two elder daughters try to persuade her to come to reason. Attendants!

ATTENDANTS. *(Kneeling)* Yes, Excellency!

WANG. Request Madam to come here.

ATTENDANTS. *(Rising)* Yes, Excellency. *(They go up* R. *and up* L., *face off* R. *and call)* His Excellency requests the presence of Madam.

MADAM. *(Off* R.*)* Yes, I will come. *(MUSIC starts.* IST *and* 2D MAIDS *enter from* R. *Go to down* R. IST MAID *crosses front to down* L. 2D MAID *stays down* R. MADAM *follows them in to down* C. *Curtseys to audience.* ATTENDANTS *return to down* L. *and down* R. *MUSIC stops.)* I am Chen, the wife of the Prime Minister, Wang. *(She turns up; steps over threshold; curtseys to* WANG*)* My respects to

Your Excellency. (PROPERTY MAN L. *places arm-chair* L. *of* WANG.)

WANG. And mine to you. Be seated. *(She sits* L. *of* WANG. MAIDS *cross to down* C. *Step over thres-hold.* IST MAID *goes* L. 2D MAID *goes* R. *to stand over* MADAM'S *chair.)*

MADAM. May I know what is your wish in asking me to come to see you in the garden?

WANG. Today is New Year's Day. I want to cele-brate it in some way. It looks as if it is going to snow. I propose that we have a feast here in the garden to enjoy the snow. And during the feast I hope you will try your best to persuade our youngest daughter to consent to marry one of the young nobles whose suit I have approved.

MADAM. Your orders will be obeyed. But I am afraid it will not be of any use, for the young minx is very obstinate. She insists on being allowed to choose for herself.

WANG. Nonsense! It is scandalous for a young girl to choose a husband herself. Our young genera-tion is becoming hopeless. What are the teachings of Confucius and Mencius coming to? They study them and then act in defiance of them. *(He shows a trifle of anger.)*

MADAM. She says that "Not to impose your will upon others" is one of the most important teachings of Confucius and she hopes you will not forget it.

WANG. *(Blowing his long beard in a rage)* Ph-ew! You have utterly spoiled her. For heaven's sake do not encourage her to rebel against me. *(He turns aside and calls)* Attendants!

ATTENDANTS. *(Kneeling)* Yes, Excellency!

WANG. Tell General Su, General Wei, and the ladies to come here at once.

ATTENDANTS. Yes, Excellency! *(They rise, cross up* R. *and* L. *and call off* R. *aloud:)* His Excellency

asks General Su and General Wei and his three
daughters to come to see him.

VOICES. Yes, we are coming.

(MUSIC starts. MADAM *receives cup of tea from*
   PROPERTY MAN L., *gives it to* WANG, *who drinks
   and returns cup to* MADAM. *She returns it to*
   PROPERTY MAN, *who retires to his place. During the above business* SU *has entered up* R., *followed by* WEI. SU *to down* L.C. WEI *to down*
   R.C. BOTH *face audience. MUSIC stops.)*

SU. *(Bows)* Your humble servant, Su, the Dragon General.

WEI. *(Bows)* Wei, the Tiger General, at your
service. (PROPERTY MAN R. *places two chairs* R. *of*
WANG.)

SU. *(He and* WEI *face each other)* Just a moment
ago our father-in-law, the Prime Minister, asked
us to come to the garden to see him. I wonder what
is the reason.

WEI. So do I. Let us go up and find out. *(Bows.)*

SU. *(Stretching out his* R. *arm. Bows)* You first.
(They enter together and bow to WANG.)

SU *and* WEI. *(Bowing)* Your sons-in-law beg to
pay their respects to you.

WANG *and* MADAM. Don't stand on ceremony, but
please be seated.

SU *and* WEI. Thank you! *(MUSIC starts. They
move* R., *bow to each other, sit,* SU *next to* WANG,
WEI R. *of* SU.)

(GOLDEN STREAM *and* SILVER STREAM *enter up* R.
   *They pause at entrance and business of arrang-
   ing hair. They come down* C.; *curtsey to audience. MUSIC stops.)*

GOLDEN STREAM. *(*L.C. *to audience)* Your humble

maid, Golden Stream, the eldest daughter of the Wang family. My husband is Su, the Dragon General. (PROPERTY MAN L. *places two chairs* L. *of* MADAM.)

SILVER STREAM. *(*R.C. *to audience)* The second daughter, Silver Stream, at your service. My husband is Wei, the Tiger General, and the most handsome man in the kingdom. When we were talking in the reception room our father called us to come here. *(She peeps over her shoulder, looking* R. *and* L.*)* It seems there is going to be a family council, and I believe I know the reason why. *(The* TWO SISTERS *now face each other)* My eldest sister. *(Curtsey.)*

GOLDEN STREAM. Yes, my youngest sister. *(Curtsey.)*

SILVER STREAM. Do you know why father has called us to come here?

GOLDEN STREAM. No, I don't know.

SILVER STREAM. *(Speaking very rapidly)* Because of our minx of a sister. I'm sure it's about her— She is not very young now and she is choosing a husband for herself. No wonder. I would do the same if I were in her place. But Father is also choosing one for her, and no wonder. I would do the same if I were in his place. And Mother—

GOLDEN STREAM. *(Interrupting her)* All right, don't talk so much. Let us go in. *(They enter up to* WANG *and* MADAM; *curtsey.)*

GOLDEN STREAM *and* SILVER STREAM. *(Together)* Your daughters have come to pay their respects to you, dear Father and Mother.

WANG *and* MADAM. Don't stand on ceremony. Be seated.

GOLDEN STREAM *and* SILVER STREAM. Thank you. *(They* BOTH *sit,* GOLDEN STREAM *next to* MADAM, SILVER STREAM L. *of* GOLDEN STREAM.*)*

SILVER STREAM. *(Quick and sharp)* Are you calling us here to discuss the case of my youngest sister, Precious Stream?

WANG. Eh—yes; no, not exactly. Today is New Year's Day. I want to celebrate it in some way. It looks as if it is going to snow. I propose that we have a feast here in the garden to enjoy the snow. And during the feast, well—

SILVER STREAM. Oh, I know! And during the feast we will try our best to persuade our youngest sister to consent to marry one of the young nobles whose suit you have approved. Isn't that so?

WANG. Yes, that is exactly what I wish you to do.

GOLDEN STREAM. But if she has a suitor in her own mind—

WANG. Nonsense, I won't allow it.

GOLDEN STREAM. Is that fair, dear Father?

MADAM. Yes, is that fair, dear?

WANG. Well—a daughter's duty is to obey.

SILVER STREAM. Father knows everything of consequence, and if our youngest sister's secret suitor is a desirable person, then he must be on father's list. Otherwise, it must be some unsuitable creature whom it would be well and proper to avoid. When I was young I left my choice entirely in dear father's hands, and, you see, I became the wife of the most handsome man in the kingdom. *(Rises, curtseys, and sits.)*

WEI. Oh, I thank you. *(Hides face with sleeve.)*

GOLDEN STREAM. *(Sarcastically)* But Father can't find another man as handsome as your husband for her now.

WEI. Yes, that's true.

SILVER STREAM. Not another word, please. She is coming. *(MUSIC starts. PROPERTY MAN L. places chair L. for PRECIOUS STREAM.)*

(PRECIOUS STREAM *enters up* R., *preceded by* MAID.

MAID *to* R.C. PRECIOUS STREAM *does business of arranging hair, then down to* C. *MUSIC stops.)*

PRECIOUS STREAM. I am your humble maid, Precious Stream, the third and youngest daughter of the Wang family. When I was doing my embroidery work in my boudoir I heard my father calling to me to come to the garden to see him. My maid, lead the way to the garden.

MAID. Yes, my lady.

(MAID *enters the garden and goes* L., *followed by* PRECIOUS STREAM. PRECIOUS STREAM *up* C. *to* WANG; *curtseys.)*

PRECIOUS STREAM. Your daughter's respects to you, dear Father and Mother.

WANG *and* MADAM. Don't stand on ceremony. Be seated.

PRECIOUS STREAM. Thank you. And my compliments to my brothers-in-law and my dear sisters. *(Sits* L. 3D MAID *crosses behind* PRECIOUS STREAM'S *chair.* ATTENDANTS *close door and cross up* R. *to behind chairs.)*

ALL. Thank you. The same to you.

PRECIOUS STREAM. May I know why I am called to come here, dear Father?

WANG. Yes. Ahem! Well—the fact is—eh—today—eh—today is—eh—

SILVER STREAM. Allow me, Father. *(Rapidly, as if reciting a poem)* Today is New Year's Day. Father wants to celebrate it in some way. It looks as if it's going to snow. Father proposes that we have a feast here in the garden to enjoy the snow. And during the feast he wishes—

WANG. *(Uneasily)* Ahem!—Ahem! That will do, thank you.

PRECIOUS STREAM. Splendid. Call the servants to

arrange the table at once. And when the snow is falling we shall have the gentlemen to write poems for the occasion. I think my brothers-in-law will be glad to do so.

SU *and* WEI. *(Looking at each other and shaking heads)* No.

WANG. Attendants! (ATTENDANTS *come down* R. *and* L. *and kneel.)*

ATTENDANTS. Yes, Excellency.

WANG. Remove that big rock to the centre, and let it serve as our table. *(Points to table down* L.*)*

ATTENDANTS. Yes, Excellency. *(They go to table* L., ONE *above and* ONE *below it. They try to lift it, pause, take breath, try again, but are unable to move it. Kneel)* Excellency, the rock refuses to be moved!

WANG. Nonsense! What useless creatures you are! (ATTENDANTS *cross up* L., *returning to places up* L. *and up* R.*)*

MADAM. But, my dear, it is too heavy for them.

WEI. Cowards! If it refuses to be moved why don't you kick it?

SILVER STREAM. Yes, why don't you kick it?

PRECIOUS STREAM. Dear Father, I do think it's too heavy for them. Why don't you ask my brothers-in-law to remove it? They are renowned all the world over for their strength. It would be real sport.

WEI. My dear relative, as our greatest sage, Confucius, said: "To kill a little chicken, why use a big knife which is made for killing horses!"

WANG. *(Correcting him)* "—for killing oxen" is the ancient text.

WEI. So, to lift this little rock is too small a feat for me. It is also beneath my dignity. If there were a big rock, say ten times as large as that, or even larger, then I would do it with pleasure, and with great ease, I assure you.

SILVER STREAM. Yes, I can assure you, too.

Su. *(A more truthful and practical man)* As none of us can remove that rock, may I make a suggestion?

Wang. Certainly.

All. Yes.

Su. You know the gardener, Hsieh Ping-Kuei, before coming into our service was a street acrobat. I remember having seen him perform wonderful feats of strength by lifting up huge stones. Now I—

Wei. Yes, I saw him lifting up a stone ten times as big as that one. Order him to remove it for us.

Silver Stream. Yes, order him to do it.

Precious Stream. Then don't you think this rock is too small for him?

Wang. Attendants! *(Attendants come down L. and R. and kneel.)*

Attendants. Yes, Excellency.

Wang. Order the gardener, Hsieh Ping-Kuei, to come here at once.

Attendants. Yes, Excellency. *(Both go up L. and R. and call off L.)* His Excellency orders the gardener, Hsieh Ping-Kuei, to come here at once.

Hsieh. *(Off stage)* His Excellency's orders will be obeyed. *(Attendants move to their places L. and R. behind chairs.)*

(Hsieh enters up L.; gets book from Property Man. Down to C.; addresses audience.)

Hsieh. I am your humble servant, Hsieh Ping-Kuei, once a beggar, now the gardener to His Excellency the Prime Minister Wang. There is very little work to be done here, so I am always reading, hoping to make up the time I wasted in my youth. I hear that His Excellency is calling me. Let me go inside and see what are his orders. *(He puts the book down his back. Enters garden and kneels be-*

fore WANG, R.C.*)* Your humble gardener, Hsieh Ping-Kuei, begs to report himself for Your Excellency's orders.

WANG. I want you to remove that rock to the centre.

MADAM. It will serve as a table, you see.

HSIEH. Very well, Your Excellency. *(He goes to table, picks it up, raises it up* L. *and behind row of chairs. He stumbles and almost falls.)*

ALL. *(Startled)* Oooooooooooo— (HSEIH *brings table to in front of* WANG *at* C.*)*

HSIEH. Is that all right, Your Excellency?

WANG. All right. You may go now. (HSIEH *crosses* L.; *as he passes* PRECIOUS STREAM:)

PRECIOUS STREAM. All of us, and especially General Wei, thank you very much. (HSIEH *bows.)* That will do. You may go now. *(He goes off up* L.*)*

WEI. That's nothing. I can easily remove a rock ten times larger.

WANG. Attendants!

ATTENDANTS. *(Coming down* L. *and down* R., *kneeling)* Yes, Excellency.

WANG. Serve the feast here. *(MUSIC starts.)*

ATTENDANTS. *(Rising)* Yes, Excellency.

(PROPERTY MAN R. *gives tray with wine jug and seven cups on it to* ATTENDANT R., *who carries it* C.; *gives it to* ATTENDANT L., *who puts it on table before* WANG.)

WANG. *(Rising. MUSIC softer)* Precious Stream, my dear daughter, serve the wine. *(MUSIC louder.* PRECIOUS STREAM *pours wine. MUSIC softer.)* Madam, my honorable sons-in-law, my dear daughters, please drink. *(MUSIC louder. As he names them they come forward to table and pick up wine cups together.)*

ALL. Thank you. *(They drink. MUSIC softer.)*

WANG. The wine is excellent. Now once more. *(MUSIC louder. PRECIOUS STREAM repeats pouring business.)*

ALL. Thank you. *(They drink. As they are drinking, the PROPERTY MEN bring chairs down L. and down R., face C., standing on chairs, unfurl flags and allow snow to fall, then return chairs and retire to their places. MUSIC stops.)*

WANG. What a beautiful scene the snow makes. *(ALL sit.)* Having wine and snow, we must also have some poems to celebrate the occasion. Who is going to write them? *(Looks to sons-in-law. PROPERTY MAN R. takes away wine jug and tray. PROPERTY MAN L. takes away table.)*

SU. I am a very poor scholar, my dear Father-in-law, and I must ask you to excuse me.

GOLDEN STREAM. Father will of course excuse you.

WEI. Although I am known as the most brilliant scholar, my dear Father-in-law, I regret to say that I am not in the right mood for poetry now. I remember some poet said: "To write good poems, one needs perspiration!" It is very cold now, you see. We can't expect any perspiration until summer comes. *(ALL except WANG and SILVER STREAM smile. SILVER STREAM is upset.)*

WANG. Perspiration? You mean inspiration.

PRECIOUS STREAM. If it's only perspiration you need, then you must be the greatest poet of the age.

WEI. Oh, thank you.

SILVER STREAM. For shame to chaff my dear one like this.

SU. As none of us can write any poetry, may I make another suggestion?

ALL. Yes.

WANG. Certainly.

SU. I remember having heard the gardener, Hsieh

Ping-Kuei, sing beautiful songs in the street, and
I was told they were composed by himself.

GOLDEN STREAM. Yes, I remember, too.

WEI. No, I don't think he composed them.

WANG. Yes, he did, and that's why I took a fancy
to him, and gave him the post of my gardener as a
just reward for his talent.

WEI. Truly, you are the most just Prime Minister in history. Now let him repay some of your
kindness by entertaining us with his songs.

SILVER STREAM. Yes, if he really can.

WANG. Attendants!

ATTENDANTS. Yes, Excellency. *(They come down
L. and R. and kneel.)*

WANG. Order the gardener, Hsieh Ping-Kuei, to
come here again.

ATTENDANTS. Yes, Excellency. *(Go up L. and R.
Call off L.)* His Excellency orders the gardener,
Hsieh Ping-Kuei, to come here again.

HSIEH. *(Off stage)* Coming. (ATTENDANTS *retire
to their places.* HSIEH *enters up L., returns book to*
PROPERTY MAN *and comes to below* PRECIOUS
STREAM'S *chair, and kneels.)*

WANG. As we are drinking wine and enjoying the
snow here, we find we need a little poem to celebrate the occasion. As I have heard that you are
somewhat of a poet in your own way, I order you
to give us one of your poems.

HSIEH. If Your Excellency will excuse my being
forward—

WANG. Certainly.

HSIEH. I must beg to point out to Your Excellency that I am one of your laborers and my duty
to Your Excellency is limited to labor.

WEI. Bravo! I said he couldn't!

SILVER STREAM. So did I.

SU. Wait a moment. What do you mean?

GOLDEN STREAM. Tell us candidly.

HSIEH. If it is not my labor but my talent you want, then I must beg you to treat me as a gentleman and I must be invited, not ordered.

WEI. Impossible! What impudence!

SILVER STREAM. The man ought to be thrashed.

PRECIOUS STREAM. Why, this is most reasonable. A true poet must not be treated as a workman. Why shouldn't we treat him with proper respect?

WANG. Well, to show that I am a just man I will give you a seat in that corner, and request you to write a short poem of four lines on the subject of "Wine, Snow and Poetry." If your poem proves to be good, I will give you a reward; if your poem is bad, or you can't write at all—

WEI. I'll have him punished for his impudence.

SILVER STREAM. That's exactly my view.

WANG. Do you hear, man?

HSIEH. Yes, Your Excellency. *(He rises, crosses to down L. and calls)* Attendants, bring me pen, inkstone and paper.

WEI. What insolence!

WANG. Really, this is too much! (PROPERTY MAN L. *gives pen, inkstone and paper on tray to* PRECIOUS STREAM'S 3D MAID.)

PRECIOUS STREAM. Why, this is but the true attitude of a poet. If no one will bring you what you want, allow me. *(MUSIC starts.* PRECIOUS STREAM *rises and goes to* HSIEH. MAID *follows to* PRECIOUS STREAM'S R. PROPERTY MAN L. *brings* PRECIOUS STREAM'S *chair to* HSIEH. *He sits.* PRECIOUS STREAM *prepares ink on inkstone; points the pen; hands paper to* HSIEH; *gives him prepared pen. She gets behind chair.* MAID *to her* L. MUSIC *stops.)*

HSIEH. *(As he writes)*
"Wine brings a double cheer if snow be here."

WANG.
"Wine brings a double cheer if snow be here."

HSIEH.

"Snow takes a brighter white from song's delight."

WANG.

"Snow takes a brighter white from song's delight."

HSIEH.

"Ah, but when cups abound, and song is sweet,
And snow is falling 'round, the joy's complete."

WANG. "—the joy's complete."

*(While this is being written, ALL nod their heads in
time to the rhythm, with the exception of WEI.
PRECIOUS STREAM takes back pen; gives it to
MAID; returns to her place. MAID follows.
HSIEH rises; crosses to WANG. PROPERTY MAN
L. brings back PRECIOUS STREAM's chair and
takes tray from MAID.)*

HSIEH. Here you are, Your Excellency. *(Hands
him the paper and backs to down L.)*

WANG. Well, it is very good indeed. *(Passes paper
to SU.)*

SU. Yes, very good. *(Tries to pass paper to WEI.)*

WEI. I don't think so. I could write a much better
poem.

SILVER STREAM. Yes, I'm sure you could.

WANG. *(To HSIEH)* Thank you. You may go now.
A reward will be given to you—later on.

MADAM. I will order the steward to give it to
you.

HSIEH. *(Bowing)* Many thanks, Your Excellency.
(Starts to leave.)

WANG. *(To his wife)* You see, my dear, our family needs a poet. *(At this point HSIEH stops; bows
to PRECIOUS STREAM. WANG sees and is indignant.
HSIEH exits up L.)* When we want to celebrate an
occasion like this we find that none of our family
can write anything. Now those suitors whom I have

approved all write first-class poems. All the poems they have shown to me are excellent.

PRECIOUS STREAM. My brother-in-law, Wei, also used to show you very good poems before he married my sister.

WEI. I can still show you good poems if I am allowed.

SILVER STREAM. Yes, I am sure he can.

PRECIOUS STREAM. I should like to see you write them in my presence.

WEI. Impossible!

SILVER STREAM. Imposs— (ALL *snicker*.)

WANG. How unreasonable! But these young suitors are also all rich and of high birth; indeed, one couldn't find anyone better than they are in every way.

PRECIOUS STREAM. May I ask you, dear Father, is every one of them rich and noble?

WANG. Yes, certainly.

PRECIOUS STREAM. Are there not one or two among them not so rich and noble?

WANG. No. None. They are all equally rich and equally noble.

PRECIOUS STREAM. (*Rises and curtseys*) Then, dear Father, how can I choose? By choosing one, it will be unfair to the others. To be fair, I think I must refuse them all. (*She sits.*)

WANG. Oh! (*He puts his hand to his forehead.*)

MADAM. (*Laughs*) You have outwitted your father, dear child.

GOLDEN STREAM. Very clever indeed.

SILVER STREAM. Very silly.

PRECIOUS STREAM. (*Coaxingly*) Dear Father, you are the Prime Minister and therefore the most clever man in the kingdom. (WANG *is rather flattered and looks pleased.*) When the most clever man in the kingdom is at a loss as to say who is the most suitable, then how can I, a stupid young girl without any experience, make a decision?

MADAM. That's true.

GOLDEN STREAM. Yes, dear Father, it's quite true.

SILVER STREAM. No! When I was young I was neither stupid nor without experience. (ALL *react*.)

WEI. Why don't you refer the matter to the imperial counsellors, so that they may hold a conference?

SU. Nonsense! Our dear Father-in-law will settle it sooner or later. In the meantime, let us drop it.

PRECIOUS STREAM. *(She rises; curtseys)* Thank you, dear Brother-in-law! *(Sits.* SU *smiles at her, rises and bows.)*

WANG. *(Rises)* I think I have a very good plan for settling it.

ALL. Marvelous! How clever! So soon!

WANG. Listen, my dear. On your birthday, the second of February, there will be a festival. Let us build a beautiful pavilion here in the garden, and let all the suitors come beneath it. You, in the pavilion, take an embroidered ball and throw it down from the pavilion. The one who catches it will be your bridegroom.

PRECIOUS STREAM. Is that a wise way to settle such a problem?

WANG. It is the only way. And I am quite determined. *(Sits.)*

MADAM. It is romantic too.

ALL. Yes, very romantic.

PRECIOUS STREAM. When even careful judgment is not sufficient to settle such a problem, is it wise to settle it by lottery?

WANG. It will not be a lottery. It will be the will of God.

WEI. The suitor who is hit by the embroidered ball can well call his case one of *force majeure. (He laughs.* SILVER STREAM *laughs also,* MADAM *looks at* WEI, *who stops. Then at* SILVER STREAM, *who also stops laughing.)*

MADAM. I see! Whenever we find a situation which cannot be dealt with by mortals we ask the help of God. We always turn to God when we are in distress.

ALL. *(Put up* R. *hands to face and say)* La, Mo, Gno, Me, To Fu.

MADAM. Well, now that we have put our responsibility upon God, shall we retire?

WANG. Yes, let us retire.

(MUSIC starts. ATTENDANTS *open doors and stand aside.* ALL *rise.* WANG *down* C., *followed by* MADAM. *He bows to audience and goes off up* L. *She curtseys and follows him, then the* TWO MAIDS *follow her.* ALL *step over threshold as on entering. As family moves downstage,* PROPPERTY MEN R. *and* L. *place chairs* R. *and* L. *in their original places. MUSIC softer.)*

SU. We have some business at my house if you will excuse us— *(He and* GOLDEN STREAM *bow and curtsey to audience and exit up* L.—*he first, she following him.* WEI *crosses to* PRECIOUS STREAM.*)*

WEI. Now, dear Sister-in-law, allow me to give you a little advice.

PRECIOUS STREAM. *(Pointing out to audience)* Look, there is a rock ten times as large as the one used for our table. I think you said a moment ago you could lift such a rock with ease. Now, will you please— *(*SILVER STREAM *to* L. *of him; pulls his sleeve.)*

WEI. I think we have some important business waiting for us, too. Good morning.

(MUSIC louder. WEI *and* SILVER STREAM *down* C., *bow and curtsey to audience and exit up* L. AT-

TENDANTS *follow them and close doors of gar-*
den. Exit up L. PROPERTY MAN L. *places chair*
C. *MUSIC stops.)*

PRECIOUS STREAM. *(Goes* R.*)* What *shall* I do?
(Goes L.*)* What shall I do? *(Taps her forehead,
then up* C.; *sits)* My maid—ask the gardener, Hsieh
Ping-Kuei, to come to me.

MAID. Yes, my lady. *(To up* L. *and calls)* Lady
Precious Stream wishes the gardener, Hsieh Ping-
Kuei, to come here immediately.

HSIEH. *(Off stage)* Yes, I am coming. (MAID *to*
L. *of* PRECIOUS STREAM. HSIEH *enters up* L. *and
kneels* L. *before* PRECIOUS STREAM*)* May I know
your orders, my lady?

PRECIOUS STREAM. Stand up, please. *(He rises.)*
My maid, provide a seat for Mr. Hsieh. (PROPERTY
MAN L. *places chair behind* HSIEH.)

HSIEH. How can I sit down before you, my lady?

PRECIOUS STREAM. The best of manners is obe-
dience.

HSIEH. *(Bows and sits)* Then I must thank you.

PRECIOUS STREAM. My maid, go to my boudoir
and fetch some fifty taels of silver for me. (MAID
curtseys and goes down C.*)* Go as quickly as possible. (MAID *opens door, goes* C., *closes door and
stoops as if listening.* PRECIOUS STREAM *comes down*
C., *opens the door and says)* And return as slowly
as possible.

MAID. *(Jumps up, moves* L. *and says)* Yes, my
lady. *(Exits up* L.*)*

PRECIOUS STREAM. *(Returns and sits)* Mr. Hsieh,
I now know that you are a man of both high literary
and military abilities. I wish to help you, but first
of all you must tell me about your family.

HSIEH. Thank you, my lady. Do you really want
to know about my family? Well, I am of a very **poor**
family.

PRECIOUS STREAM. That I know. I want to hear about the members of your family.

HSIEH. My father and mother are both dead.

PRECIOUS STREAM. I see. Is there anyone else in your family?

HSIEH. Being poor, I only had one father and one mother!

PRECIOUS STREAM. I mean those of your own generation.

HSIEH. I had a brother who died at five. I have no sister.

PRECIOUS STREAM. Did any one of your family marry?

HSIEH. Yes.

PRECIOUS STREAM. *(Taken aback)* Oh! Who?

HSIEH. Well, my father married my mother.

PRECIOUS STREAM. *(Relieved)* Of course! And your brother?

HSIEH. As he died at five he did not marry.

PRECIOUS STREAM. I see. Well—and did—did your parents have a daughter-in-law at all?

HSIEH. No, they had none.

PRECIOUS STREAM. Then I have something to tell you, but I find it hard to do so. *Well*, do you understand riddles?

HSIEH. A little.

PRECIOUS STREAM. On the second of February it will be my sixteenth birthday, and I am going to marry the man who is hit by the embroidered ball which I shall throw down from a beautiful pavilion to be erected here. It will be a case of the will of God, but I have resolved to take it into my own hands. I have in mind a suitable person. Now, this person, if you look far—

HSIEH. *(Continuing her speech)* —is a thousand miles away—

PRECIOUS STREAM. Yes, and if you look near—

HSIEH. Then he is before you! *(Rises.)*

PRECIOUS STREAM. Thank you! That is exactly what I mean. (MAID *enters up* R.; *comes downstage; takes silver from* PROPERTY MAN R.)

HSIEH. If my lady bestows on me such an honor I will never fail her.

PRECIOUS STREAM. My maid is returning. Not another word. Be sure to be present on the second of February. (MAID *opens door.*)

HSIEH. The second of February.

MAID. (*Up to* R. *of* PRECIOUS STREAM) Here you are, my lady.

PRECIOUS STREAM. Give it to Mr. Hsieh. (MAID *crosses to* HSIEH *and gives him the piece of silver, then stands up* L. *of* PRECIOUS STREAM.)

HSIEH. Thank you. I shall never forget your kindness. (*Down* C.) The second of February. (*Goes up* L., *gives* PROPERTY MAN *the piece of silver and exits.*)

PRECIOUS STREAM. (*Rises*) Let's retire to our boudoir and wait for the will of God. (*Exits up* L.)

3D MAID. (*Crosses down* C. *to audience*) The will of God.

(*MUSIC starts.* MAID *laughs; moves up* L., *laughing as she exits. MUSIC stops. LIGHTS fade. LIGHTS UP immediately after they have come down. MUSIC starts.*)

(*During the exit of the* MAID *and the entrance of* WANG *the* PROPERTY MAN L. *places the two chairs* L.C. *and* R.C. *with backs to audience.* PROPERTY MAN R. *places armchair* C. *for* WANG. PROPERTY MAN L. *goes off up* L. *and returns with table, which he places between the* L.C. *and* R.C. *chairs.* PROPERTY MAN R. *goes off* R. *and brings on embroidery attached to bamboo sticks. This he and* PROPERTY MAN L. *tie to outside of the two chairs. Enter* ATTENDANTS *up*

R., followed by WANG. ATTENDANTS *cross to down* R. *and* L., WANG *to down* C.*)*

WANG. Today is the second of February, the day on which I am going to take a new son-in-law into my family. *(Crosses up* C. *and sits)* I have been looking forward to it enormously, and I am very happy to find the weather is so fine. It is now quite near the hour of throwing the ball, and I must give the necessary instructions. Attendants!

ATTENDANTS. *(Kneeling)* Yes, Excellency.

WANG. You must stay in the garden and guard the gate. Admit only those young gentlemen you know I like.. *(Enter* FOUR SUITORS *from* R.—IST *and* 2D *to down* L.C., 3D *and* 4TH *to down* R.C.*)* As soon as the embroidered ball has been thrown I will come back at once.

ATTENDANTS. *(Rising)* Yes, Excellency.

IST SUITOR. *(To audience, bowing)* Lady Precious Stream is as beautiful as the flowers of May.

2D SUITOR. *(Same business)* The second of February is her wedding day.

3D SUITOR. *(Same business)* The young suitors come here happy and gay!

4TH SUITOR. *(Same business)* Who will be the lucky one—

WANG. *(Rises)* Nobody can say. *(He exits up* L. PROPERTY MAN R. *removes armchair from* C.*)*

IST SUITOR. Here we have arrived. Let us knock at the gate. *(They turn and knock at gate.)*

IST ATTENDANT. Yes, I am coming. *(He opens the door, coming* C. *with* 2D ATTENDANT*)* Good morning, my young lords. Have you young gentlemen come to await the lucky ball?

SUITORS. Exactly.

IST ATTENDANT. Come in, please. (IST ATTENDANT *shows the way to the* L., *round stage, below pavilion to* R., *they imitating his movements.*

2D ATTENDANT *closes door.* BOTH *return to places down* R. *and down* L.)

ALL. Lady Precious Stream is coming. *(MUSIC starts.)*

(PRECIOUS STREAM *enters up* R. *Two* MAIDS *before and two* MAIDS *after her. She goes to* C., *two* MAIDS R. *and two* MAIDS L. *of her—*ALL *stand facing her. She carries an embroidered ball given her by* PROPERTY MAN R. *MUSIC stops.)*

PRECIOUS STREAM. Time flies and today is the fatal day of the second of February. Although I am anxious to be free from suspense, the idea of going up to the pavilion and throwing down the embroidered ball while the crowd looks on makes me feel very shy, and I don't know how I shall ever manage to carry on. My maids!

MAIDS. Yes, my lady. *(Curtsey.)*

PRECIOUS STREAM. Lead the way to the pavilion, please.

MAIDS. Yes, my lady. *(Curtsey.)*

(MUSIC starts. The two MAIDS L. *come* C. *and go round stage, below the pavilion, followed by the two* MAIDS R. PRECIOUS STREAM *follows them. They go round stage once, then up behind pavilion.* PRECIOUS STREAM *goes in the pavilion. MUSIC stops.)*

PRECIOUS STREAM. *(Surveying the crowd represented by the* SUITORS*)* Now I must look carefully. There are princes dressed in red and there are young nobles dressed in blue. Those clad in—*(As the costume of each* SUITOR *is mentioned he steps out of line and then back)*—yellow are the sons of rich merchants, and those in white are heirs to the great land-owners! I must find where Hsieh Ping-Kuei is standing. I have looked from East to West, and now I must look from North to South. Again and again I have looked for him, and nowhere is he to be seen. I remember clearly when I gave him the silver I told him to come on this day and he promised he would. But he has proved unfaithful. *(Then to* SUITORS, *directly)* Oh, woe is me! I must retire without throwing the ball. (HSIEH *enters up* L.· *crosses down* L.)

1ST SUITOR. No! You mustn't go back.

2D SUITOR. Throw the ball before you go, please.

3D SUITOR. How can you desert us?

4TH SUITOR. I have been waiting all the morning.

PRECIOUS STREAM. Ah! I see him emerging from that corner. *(Speaks to the* SUITORS*)* Now, gentlemen, please come near to the pavilion and listen to my words. (SUITORS *one step forward.)* I want all of you to pledge your word of honor to me that you will uphold the man who, by the will of God, is going to be my husband, whoever he may be. And, moreover, that you will swear that you, one and all, will draw your swords against him who will not uphold the destined match.

ALL. We swear! *(Step back.)*

PRECIOUS STREAM. This marriage is to be arranged by the will of God, and we mortals have to abide by this arrangement. Now, catch the ball. *(She holds ball above her head; swings it; counts)* One, two, three! (SUITORS *sway and reach upward each time she counts. She throws ball and* HSIEH *catches it.)*

HSIEH. Here it is!

SUITORS. Oh! *(They make a move forwards.)*

PRECIOUS STREAM. Gentlemen, remember that all of you have pledged your word of honor to me and you must abide by it. Now, like decent folk, congratulate him and me.

ALL. Congratulations!

HSIEH. Thanks.

(PRECIOUS STREAM *has now got down from the pa-*
vilion. Curtseys to HSIEH, *then up to* SUITORS
R. *When* PRECIOUS STREAM *gets down from*
pavilion, PROPERTY MAN L. *takes table off up* L.,
returns, unties the pavilion. Takes chairs to L.
PROPERTY MAN R. *takes pavilion to* R., *then*
returns to his position R.)

SUITORS. Our hearty congratulations!
PRECIOUS STREAM. Many thanks!

(WANG *enters up* R. ; *downstage to* C.)

WANG. Where is my new son-in-law? Where is
my new son-in-law? (*Business of* SUITORS *in rota-*
tion, up stage to down stage, turning back on
WANG.)
HSIEH. At your service, my dear Father-in-law.
(WANG *sees* HSIEH—*blows through beard.* PROP-
ERTY MAN R. *brings cushion forward and catches*
WANG *as he faints.* WANG *faints into the arms of*
PROPERTY MEN, *who lower him onto the stage.*
PRECIOUS STREAM *fans him with her sleeve.*)
PRECIOUS STREAM. Oh, Father, Father!
SUITORS. (*Fanning* WANG *with sleeves*) Oh, Your
Excellency! Your Excellency!
WANG. (PROPERTY MEN *pick him up*) Oh, my
God!
PRECIOUS STREAM. Yes, dear Father, this is in-
deed the will of God.
SUITORS. (*Sarcastically*) The will of God!
WANG. (*To audience*) But I won't have it. I will
take the matter away from God into my own hands.
PRECIOUS STREAM. But, Father, aren't you glad?
You said our family needed a poet, and now we

have one. *(Crosses L. to* HSIEH*)* God has granted your wish.

WANG. We will see whether God will grant me a different wish.

PRECIOUS STREAM. Now, my gallant suitors, did you not swear that you would draw your swords against him who dared not to uphold the destined match?

SUITORS. Yes, we did. *(One step forward, brave-ly.)*

WANG. *(To* SUITORS*)* What! (SUITORS *fall back.* WANG *turns to* PRECIOUS STREAM*)* You have con-spired against your own father.

PRECIOUS STREAM. I never dreamt it would be you we should have to deal with.

WANG. *(To* SUITORS*)* You fools, to think that I once liked you! I am a blind fool. Now get out, all of you. (ATTENDANTS *open doors.* HSIEH *and* PRE-CIOUS STREAM *go up to entrance L. and take tea from the* PROPERTY MAN. WANG *takes* SUITORS *one by one by the ear and ushers them out up* R.*)*

1ST SUITOR. Lady Precious Stream is as beautiful as the flowers in May.

2D SUITOR. The second of February is her wed-ding day.

3D SUITOR. The young suitors come here happy and gay.

4TH SUITOR. But when they are leaving they say—

WANG. *(Kicking* 4TH SUITOR, *against whom* PROPERTY MAN L. *holds pillow)* Woe is the day. *(They exeunt. MUSIC starts.* PROPERTY MAN R. *places armchair* C. PROPERTY MAN L. *places two chairs L. of* WANG, *then* PRECIOUS STREAM's *chair.* PROPERTY MAN R. *places two chairs R. of* WANG. WANG *sits* C.*)*

(Enter up R. MADAM, GOLDEN STREAM, SILVER STREAM, SU *and* WEI. *They come up to* WANG,

curtsey, bow and sit. PRECIOUS STREAM *comes down* L. *to her chair; does not sit.* HSIEH *goes round back, down* R., *and stands opposite* PRECIOUS STREAM. *MUSIC stops.*)

MADAM. *(To* PRECIOUS STREAM*)* Why don't you sit down, my dear?

PRECIOUS STREAM. So long as my future husband is not given a seat, I can't sit down, dear Mother.

MADAM. Then be seated, both of you.

WANG. No! This is the house of a Prime Minister, not a beggar's hut. How can he be allowed to sit down here?

MADAM. Dear, you are only making the situation worse. Come, don't be headstrong. Let all of us sit down and talk over the matter, and see what is to be done.

WANG. *(Sulkily)* All right. Have your own way. (PROPERTY MAN R. *places chair behind* HSIEH.)

MADAM. Now be seated, please. (BOTH *sit.*)

HSIEH. Thank you, Madam.

PRECIOUS STREAM. Thank you, dear Mother.

WANG. *(Gruffly)* Say, man, on what conditions— (MADAM *nudges him. Then softly*) —will you let her be free?

WEI. Allow me to arrange for you, dear Father-in-law. I know how to deal with this sort of customer. Look here, my man! Say, my friend! Hullo, Hsieh Ping-Kuei! *(Rises)* Mr. Hsieh Ping-Kuei!

HSIEH. *(Fiercely)* What is your wish, my great General?

WEI. Don't be cross, my—er—Mr. Hsieh. You know it would never do for Lady Precious Stream to marry you, a beg— (SU *nudges* WEI.) Say—a poor man. I quite understand that this is, for you, a great chance, and that you must have a handsome price before you let go your hold.

HSIEH. *(Fiercely, rises)* I don't quite understand your meaning.

SILVER STREAM. *(Rises; goes R.)* You can't bully my husband. Bully him back, my dear. (HSIEH *turns back to* WEI.)

WEI. *(Curtly)* Be quiet—*(Softly)*—dear. (SILVER STREAM *to* L.; *curtseys and sits.)* I mean, that if you will let us off quietly, without any scandal, I am sure my father-in-law is willing to give you, say—

SILVER STREAM. One hundred taels of silver.

WEI. *(Watching* HSIEH*)* No, say two hundred.

SILVER STREAM. Not a penny more.

WANG. I am a just and generous man. I will offer you five hundred taels.

WEI. Now, be sensible, my man. *(Sits.)*

WANG. Well, how much do you want? (MADAM *presses* WANG's *arm.)* How much do you want, Mr. Hsieh?

HSIEH. I want nothing from you, sir. Even millions and billions could not buy me off. The decision lies with Lady Precious Stream. If she thinks that I am not her equal, and that this is but a lamentable mistake, just let her say the word, and I will go away without taking a penny from you.

PRECIOUS STREAM. *(Rises)* Beautiful! (HSIEH *and* PRECIOUS STREAM *sit.)*

SU. It's quite right.

MADAM. Dear, dear!

GOLDEN STREAM. He is playing the game.

WANG. My dear Daughter, you know that to me you are dearer than all. Now, say the word and let us get out of this disgrace.

WEI. And if—eh—Mr. Hsieh actually refuses to take any money, then the five hundred taels you promised, dear Father-in-law, ought to be given to me as a reward for my acting as a go-between.

SILVER STREAM. Of course Father will reward you, dear.

PRECIOUS STREAM. *(Rises.* HSIEH *rises.)* I am sorry to deprive you of your reward. I will stick to my match. (HSIEH *bows.* ALL *react.)* To my sister— *(Curtsey)* I am not worth one hundred taels, and to my brother-in-law—*(Curtsey)*—only two hundred, and even to my father—*(Curtseys)*—who professes to love me dearer than all, I am worth only five hundred.

WANG. No. *(Beckons* PRECIOUS STREAM *to him. She goes.)* In my heart I was prepared to offer one thousand.

PRECIOUS STREAM. *(Crosses back of chair)* Thank you, Father. *(To audience)* I see I am getting on. *(To* FAMILY*)* You seem to think that one would prefer to have, let us say, a thousand taels rather than to have me. And here is a man who refuses to take millions and billions and prefers me instead. Shall I be so ungrateful as to give him the go-by and to remain with those who value me so little? No, Father, I decline! *(Curtseys and sits.* HSIEH *sits.)*

GOLDEN STREAM. So would I.

MADAM. Dear, dear!

SU. Very noble!

SILVER STREAM. Very silly!

WEI. It's too bad. My five hundred taels are gone.

WANG. If you insist on marrying him, all I can say is that a beggar girl is going to marry a beggar and remain one. You need not expect any dowry from me. No—not even a penny.

PRECIOUS STREAM. *(Rises)* No, Father. Not a beggar girl to a beggar. But a working girl to a worker. We both can work.

WANG. *(Laughs)* You?—Work? Impossible!

SILVER STREAM. Don't you think it will soil your beautiful clothes?

PRECIOUS STREAM. No, because I will not wear them. *(She goes* C. *The* FAMILY *crowd round her,*

MADAM *and the* TWO DAUGHTERS L. *of her, the* MEN
R. *of her with backs to the audience.* WANG *remains
by his chair; turns his back upon them.* MADAM
helps PRECIOUS STREAM *off with her clothes; hands
them to* R. PROPERTY MAN. PRECIOUS STREAM *gives
her jewels to.* L. PROPERTY MAN. PROPERTY MAN R.
moves forward, takes PRECIOUS STREAM'S *dress and
puts it off up* R. PROPERTY MAN L. *moves forward
when* PRECIOUS STREAM *receives her jewels.*) The
ancient proverb says: "A good son will not depend
upon his father's wealth; and a good daughter will
not depend upon her family for clothes." Here I am
giving back to you these fine clothes. And here are
your jewels, too.

MADAM. Oh, dear, don't!

GOLDEN STREAM. My poor sister!

SU. A brave girl!

SILVER STREAM. I wonder how they will manage
to live.

WEI. They will soon die of starvation.

WANG. *(Still in a rage)* Do you mean that you
will leave us? Probably will come back to us when
you find you are starving. (ALL *sit except* PRECIOUS
STREAM *and* HSIEH, *whose chairs have been removed.*)

PRECIOUS STREAM. That's far from the case. If
I come back to see you, dear Mother, it will be
when we can raise our heads higher than any of
you can.

WANG. Poverty and failure will be your lot. But
don't come to me for any help.

MADAM. Don't mind what your father says, dear.
We shall always be ready to help you. But you're
not really going to leave us for good, are you?

GOLDEN STREAM. Please don't, dear Sister.

PRECIOUS STREAM. *(Crosses to* R. *below* HSIEH)
I am afraid I'll have to. My place is to be by my
husband's side for better or for worse. (PROPERTY

MAN L. *is putting cushion in front of* WANG *as* PRECIOUS STREAM *crosses to kneel.*) My dear Father, your humble daughter, Precious Stream, pays her respects——

WANG. *(Rising and snatching away pillow)* No! You needn't consider me as your father. (PROPERTY MAN L. *places second pillow.)*

PRECIOUS STREAM. *(Kneeling)* Then I must at least thank you for your share in my birth.

WANG. It was a mere accident. *(Sees* MADAM; *sits quickly.* PRECIOUS STREAM *rises and crosses to below* HSIEH *at* R.*)*

SILVER STREAM. And a sad one, too.

WANG. But I'll bet you'll be glad to leave him very soon.

PRECIOUS STREAM. Do you dare to lay a wager definitely by clapping hands three times with me, Father?

WANG. Certainly, and do you dare?

PRECIOUS STREAM. Certainly.

ALL. Oh, please don't!

PRECIOUS STREAM. *(To audience at* C.*)* I call upon all of you here to witness. Today I hereby make a wager by clapping hands with my father three times, that my husband and I will never come back to the Prime Minister's house unless we are rich and successful. (PRECIOUS STREAM *goes up to below and* R. *of* WANG. WANG *rises and they clap hands three times.* WANG *sits.* PRECIOUS STREAM *returns to below* HSIEH.)

ALL. It can't be helped now.

PRECIOUS STREAM. *(To* HSIEH*)* Now let us leave here for good and prepare for the wedding. *(They go down* C.*)*

HSIEH. *(To audience)* I will always honor you.

PRECIOUS STREAM. *(To audience)* And I will obey you.

HSIEH. *(Turns* R. *to* PRECIOUS STREAM*)* I will protect you.

PRECIOUS STREAM. *(Turns* L. *to* HSIEH*)* I will love you. (HSIEH *turns up* L. *and exits,* PRECIOUS STREAM *following.)*

WANG. *(Rising and going downstage—*MADAM *follows)* Disgraceful!

WEI. Disgusting!

SILVER STREAM. Scandalous!

WANG. Let us retire.

(MUSIC starts. They ALL *move downstage.* WANG *bows to audience and exits up* L. MADAM *follows him after curtseying.* SU *and* GOLDEN STREAM *repeat the business. Then* WEI *and* SILVER STREAM *follow.* ATTENDANTS *and* MAIDS *come last but they do not bow or curtsey.* PROPERTY MEN *replace chairs to* L. *and* R. *and retire to off up* L. *and off up* R. *MUSIC stops. LIGHTS dim.)*

END OF ACT ONE

(NO CURTAIN)

(NOTE: There is no pause between Act I and Act II. As soon as the LIGHTS have faded on Act I the READER enters immediately.)

ACT TWO

GONG #1

Enter READER *from down* L. *SPOTLIGHT on* READER.

READER. By some accident we missed the simple but romantic marriage ceremony. Perhaps we purposely avoided it because we thought it might not turn out successfully, so it would be better to have nothing to do with the matter. Nevertheless we are always desirous to hear what happened to Precious Stream and Hsieh Ping-Kuei, and so we have kept in touch with them somehow or other. We decided that we may condescend to pay them a visit. Now that their honeymoon is over we will certainly not be considered as intruders. (Even if they object to our calling, we will go and watch them afar.) We arrive at the outside of the city at an open space before a kind of cave where the newly married couple live. The open space in front of the cave and the interior of the cave are supposed to be represented here. And further, when circumstances render it necessary, the winding road on the little hill which leads to the cave is included in the scene. There is no decoration whatever on the stage and the audience must have recourse to their imagination. *(Exit* READER *down* L.)

(GONG #2. LIGHTS up. PROPERTY MEN enter from up R. and L., bow, etc. GONG #3. MUSIC starts. Enter 1ST and 2D SOLDIERS up R.; downstage to R.C. and L.C.; face each other, picking up bag of rice and firewood from PROPERTY MAN R. as they enter. MUSIC stops.)

1ST SOLDIER. Here we are.

2D SOLDIER. Yes, I believe this is the place.

1ST SOLDIER. Let us knock at the door. *(He pretends to knock. PROPERTY MAN L. knocks on his box.)* Is there anyone there? *(Backs to audience.)*

PRECIOUS STREAM. *(Off stage R.)* Yes, I am coming. *(Enters up R.; down to C.; addresses audience)* If you are rich, even the most distant relations come to visit you; if you are poor not even the closest will come near you. Since I married Hsieh Ping-Kuei we rarely have visitors. But just now I heard a strange knocking at the door. *(Calls out)* Who is knocking at the door?

1ST SOLDIER. We have brought some firewood and rice for our eldest brother Hsieh.

PRECIOUS STREAM. *(Goes round R., making a circle, as though descending steps, and comes to C. between them)* Much obliged. *(Runs to door of cave)* Please bring in what you have brought. *(They enter, and stand before her.)*

1ST SOLDIER. Here are ten hundredweight of firewood.

PRECIOUS STREAM. Put it here, please. *(PROPERTY MAN L. removes firewood.)*

2D SOLDIER. Here are five hundredweight of rice.

PRECIOUS STREAM. Put it here, please. As your eldest brother, Hsieh, is not at home, you will excuse me for not asking you to stay and drink a cup of tea. *(PROPERTY MAN R. removes rice.)*

1ST SOLDIER. Don't stand on ceremony.

2D SOLDIER. Thank you all the same.

PRECIOUS STREAM. Thank you for your trouble. I won't detain you.

1ST SOLDIER. Don't mention it. Good-bye.

2D SOLDIER. Only too delighted. Good-bye.

PRECIOUS STREAM. *(Curtseys)* Good-bye. (PROPERTY MAN L. *places chair* C. PROPERTY MAN R. *does horses' hoofs for* HSIEH's *entrance.* SOLDIERS *exit up* L. PRECIOUS STREAM *to* C.; *sits and sews.*)

HSIEH. *(Off stage* R.*)* Look out! A horse is coming! *(Enters up* R; *picks up whip from* PROPERTY MAN's *box* R. *Gallops down* R. *to* C.*)* To a newly married man an hour away from his home seems to be three years. So I feel I have been absent from my home for ages. As I have some important news for my dear wife, I must hurry on by whipping my horse. *(He goes up* L. *round stage again, coming to* C.*)* Here is my humble cave which I consider better than a splendid palace. *(He ties horse* R., *giving whip to* PROPERTY MAN R. *He calls out and knocks as though to someone in a cave)* My dear third sister, will you kindly open the door?

PRECIOUS STREAM. *(Rises; goes up* R. *and round; comes out of cave)* Is that you, my lord and master Hsieh, who has come back?

HSIEH. Yes, I have come back with some important news. (PRECIOUS STREAM *opens door. They enter cave.)*

PRECIOUS STREAM. Never mind about the news. (HSIEH *enters. They both ascend stairs.)* The most important thing is, do you want something to eat and drink? (HSIEH *sits* C., *she* L. *of him on stool placed by* PROPERTY MAN L.*)*

HSIEH. Thank you, I had a good dinner at the camp.

PRECIOUS STREAM. So that's why the two soldiers brought us ten hundredweight of firewood and five hundredweight of rice.

HSIEH. Yes, that is part of the good news, too. It

is payment in advance of my salary, and we needn't worry about our food any more.

PRECIOUS STREAM. Good news indeed!

HSIEH. I have just been appointed an officer of considerable rank.

PRECIOUS STREAM. That's fairly good.

HSIEH. You don't seem to be very enthusiastic about the good news.

PRECIOUS STREAM. Oh, yes, I am rather glad that you are now beginning to ascend the ladder of promotion. But this is only a beginning. To me, my husband ought not to be satisfied until he has at least conquered the world! *(He taps his forehead.)* And what else do you want to tell me? I perceive you've something on your mind that makes you uneasy.

HSIEH. Well, as I am now in government service, I can hardly consider myself as my own master. I am ordered abroad with the troops.

PRECIOUS STREAM. "A man's ambition cannot be limited by space," as the old proverb says. You needn't be uneasy about telling me you must leave for a time, though we have been married for a month only.

HSIEH. *(Still uneasy)* Oh, quite—quite! But the fact is—is—well, it is a very long journey. We are going on a campaign to the Western Regions.

PRECIOUS STREAM. *(Astounded)* Oh! It is a long and dangerous journey even in peaceful times; and now we are at war with them.

HSIEH. That's why I am going.

PRECIOUS STREAM. Even those who go to the Western Regions as friends seldom return— I mean, seldom return satisfied.

HSIEH. No! They never return at all.

PRECIOUS STREAM. And are you going there as their enemy?

HSIEH. Yes, our aim is to conquer them.

PRECIOUS STREAM. When do you start?

HSIEH. Very soon.

PRECIOUS STREAM. *(Rising and crossing L.)* Then I must prepare some winter clothes for you, because you may have to stay there over the New Years.

HSIEH. You needn't make any preparations for me. I have something more to tell you.

PRECIOUS STREAM. Then tell me at once. *(Sits.)*

HSIEH. It is very difficult to tell you at once.

PRECIOUS STREAM. *(Forcing a smile)* Then tell me little by little. I won't mind.

HSIEH. *(Sits)* The date of our general mobilization is fixed.

PRECIOUS STREAM. *(Anxiously)* When?

HSIEH. Well, do you understand riddles?

PRECIOUS STREAM. A little.

HSIEH. If I say the date is far, far away—

PRECIOUS STREAM. *(Forcing another smile)* A hundred years away!

HSIEH. And I say the date is quite, quite near at hand—

PRECIOUS STREAM. *(Appalled)* Today! My heaven! *(She hides her face in her long sleeves.)*

HSIEH. *(Rises; to R.; turns and faces her)* There! There! Cheer up! Wouldn't you be glad to see me return triumphantly on horseback as a General? There is something to which you may look forward.

PRECIOUS STREAM. But to think we have only been married for a month, and you are leaving me today! So unexpectedly too! Why did you apply for such a post?

HSIEH. I didn't apply for it—it was conferred upon me.

PRECIOUS STREAM. How?

HSIEH. *(Resuming his seat C.)* You know people have been talking about a monster with a red mane which has been devouring travelers in a wood near by. Well, I thought I ought to do something, and I went to the wood this morning and shot the monster, which proved to be merely a tiger of enormous size.

PRECIOUS STREAM. *(Looks at him)* A tiger of enormous size! And you say "merely."

HSIEH. Yes. I was quite disappointed.

PRECIOUS STREAM. Now, my dear hero, tell me how you did it.

HSIEH. Eh—oh—there is very little to tell. It was such a trifle. I went there. I saw a tiger. I shot it. That's all.

PRECIOUS STREAM. How fine! How grand!

HSIEH. Nonsense! Shooting an ordinary tiger when anticipating a monster is as disappointing as shooting a bird when hunting a tiger. One naturally feels a come-down. And the worst of it is that people go crazy and make a tremendous fuss about it.

PRECIOUS STREAM. And make trouble, too!

HSIEH. Yes, terrible trouble! They actually carried me to the Governor's yament, where I was appointed a Captain and ordered to join the Western Punitive Expedition. I found that Generals Wei and Su, our brothers-in-law, are the joint commanders-in-chief of this expedition, and I was ordered to mobilize with the first company immediately. *(Rises.)*

PRECIOUS STREAM. Immediately! *(Rises.)*

HSIEH. *(Gets cloth from PROPERTY MAN R.)* Yes, I was with difficulty allowed to come back to bid you a hurried good-bye, and I am afraid I have already overstayed my time. *(Rolls cloth on floor and pantomimes packing.)*

PRECIOUS STREAM. Oh, no! You mustn't leave me like this.

HSIEH. I am afraid I must. (PROPERTY MAN L. *removes chair and stool. He looks up at her)* Don't worry about me. The commanders-in-chief are our brothers-in-law, you see.

PRECIOUS STREAM. I am more worried than ever

on hearing that the wretch Wei is your chief. I don't trust him at all, and I hope you will take greatest care of yourself.

HSIEH. You needn't worry at all, for he is not going—*(He gives cloth to* PRECIOUS STREAM, *who ties it on his back)*—but staying behind to control the supply of ammunition and the paying of the soldiers. I have arranged that my pay is to be paid to you regularly in the form of rice and firewood, and he promised he would see to that. General Su will follow me with the main body of troops in a short time. *(He goes out of cave; remains* R.*)*

PRECIOUS STREAM. *(Follows him, to* L. *of him)* That is excellent. I know how to deal with the wretch Wei, and I am relieved to hear that our brother-in-law Su is going to follow you soon.

A VOICE. *(Off stage* L.*)* Dear eldest brother Hsieh, the troops are waiting for you.

HSIEH. *(Calling out)* Thank you! I will come at once. *(To* PRECIOUS STREAM*)* I must go now. My dear third Sister, allow me to salute you and bid you good-bye. *(He bows to her. She curtseys. He gets whip from* PROPERTY MAN R.*)*

PRECIOUS STREAM. I must see my hero mount his steed.

HSIEH. *(He mounts his horse)* My dear third Sister, good-bye. *(He starts going round stage, she following. Two complete circles are made.)*

PRECIOUS STREAM. Farewell! I must see you riding along the winding road to the highway.

HSIEH. You will take care of yourself for my sake, won't you?

PRECIOUS STREAM. *(Following him carefully)* Of course! And you will take care of yourself for my sake, won't you?

HSIEH. Of course! Now please go back, my dear third Sister.

PRECIOUS STREAM. No, not until we reach the highway.

HSIEH. *(Stopping down L.C., at end of second circle)* Here is the highway. Go back and have a good rest.

PRECIOUS STREAM. Do let me follow you for another short distance.

HSIEH. No, no! Although I can't bear to leave you, we must part sooner or later. The road is rough, and you are already tired. Please go back and rest.

PRECIOUS STREAM. No, no! I must see you off from the camp.

HSIEH. Impossible! That's too far for you.

PRECIOUS STREAM. I must. I must.

VOICE. *(Off stage L.)* We are starting, dear eldest brother Hsieh.

HSIEH. *(Calling out)* I come, I come! *(Pointing off R.)* Look! There is your sister, Golden Stream, coming. (PRECIOUS STREAM *looks off up R. HSIEH draws his sword and cuts the reins, the cord on the whip, then gallops off up L.)*

PRECIOUS STREAM. Oh! he has gone! *(Exits up L. MUSIC starts. MUSIC stops. LIGHTS fade. Immediately following. MUSIC starts. LIGHTS up. MADAM enters up R. with TWO ATTENDANTS preceding her, followed by DRIVER and TWO MAIDS. They come downstage. ATTENDANTS to L., MADAM C. MUSIC stops.)*

MADAM. Since the news of the death of my son-in-law, Hsieh Ping-Kuei, reached me, I have been greatly worried about my dear daughter, Precious Stream. She is very obstinate, and her pride won't allow her to accept any help from her father. It is now eight months since she left our house. As the New Year is drawing near and she is very poor, I have brought something with me and have come to pay her a visit which I ought to have done a long time ago. We must be near the place now. It's not far from here, is it, driver?

DRIVER. No, Madam.

MADAM. Faster, please.

DRIVER. Yes, Madam. *(They go round the stage once and arrive,* MADAM *standing* R.C., DRIVER *and* MAIDS *behind her to* R., ATTENDANTS L.C.)

1ST ATTENDANT. This is the cave, Madam.

MADAM. Knock at the door, please.

1ST ATTENDANT. *(Knocking)* Lady Precious Stream, please open the door.

PRECIOUS STREAM. *(Enters up* L.; *crosses to* C.) I'm coming.

1ST ATTENDANT. Madam, your mother has come to visit you. (ATTENDANTS *go* L.)

PRECIOUS STREAM. Ah, this will kill me! Oh, how can I face my mother! *(Comes out of cave.* MADAM *gets out of carriage.)* Oh, my dear, dear Mother!

MADAM. *(Puts arms round her)* My Precious Stream!

PRECIOUS STREAM. How I have longed to see you, Mother.

MADAM. And I to see you, but what a change! You, such a sweet-looking innocent little lamb, now become a hollow-faced, starved-looking, ordinary person. Oh! I cannot bear this.

PRECIOUS STREAM. Dear Mother! Allow me to kneel down and pay my respects to you.

MADAM. *(Stopping her)* No, you mustn't stand on ceremony. Attendants, draw near and pay your respects to Lady Precious Stream.

ALL. Our respects to you, Lady Precious Stream. (SERVANTS *kneel and make curtseys.)*

PRECIOUS STREAM. *(Curtseys)* Many thanks. Please don't stand on ceremony.

MADAM. Now you may all go and have a rest, but return again in a short time.

ALL. Thank you, Madam. *(They exeunt up* R.)

PRECIOUS STREAM. Oh, dear Mother, why do you condescend to come to our humble cave?

MADAM. I have heard that you are hungry and cold, and you are not well. So I wanted to see you and the place where you are living.

PRECIOUS STREAM. *(Barring the way)* Oh, no! My humble cave would profane your dignity.

MADAM. Nonsense! I must go in and see what kind of a life you are leading.

PRECIOUS STREAM. It is a poor, wretched hole, and would only make you feel uncomfortable.

MADAM. *(Firmly)* The place where my dear daughter can live for nearly a year is at least good enough for me to visit.

PRECIOUS STREAM. *(Giving in)* Then let me go in first and have the place tidied for you.

MADAM. No, I want to see it just as it is. Lead the way, my darling. *(They enter cave, PRECIOUS STREAM leading the way, taking MADAM's hand. They go round stage; finish with PRECIOUS STREAM L.C., MADAM C.)*

PRECIOUS STREAM. Mind the steps, Mother dear.

MADAM. So this is your place! (PROPERTY MAN R. *places chair* C. PROPERTY MAN L. *brings stool; places it* L. *of* MADAM.) Oh, you silly darling, fancy your forsaking your beautifully decorated boudoir and coming to this horrible cave! How could you?

PRECIOUS STREAM. *(Offering her a chair)* Make yourself comfortable in this poor chair, dear Mother. (PROPERTY MAN L. *brings bowl and chopsticks above* PRECIOUS STREAM. *She takes them from him, and gives them to* MADAM, *who gives them to* PROPERTY MAN R.) I am afraid I have no tea or refreshments to offer you, except some poor rice.

MADAM. Fancy sacrificing the delicacies you enjoyed for this poor stuff! How could you? Now, sit down yourself.

PRECIOUS STREAM. *(Sitting on the* L. *side)* Thank

you, dear Mother! After those delicacies this plain fare seemed to be very palatable to me.

MADAM. You are undernourished. That's why you are ill.

PRECIOUS STREAM. Indeed it is not a question of food. The wretched Wei told me that my husband had been killed. It was this news that sent me to bed.

MADAM. This news may be false, my darling.

PRECIOUS STREAM. Oh, yes! I don't believe it at all. But still, it makes me feel wretched. And Father sends agents to try to persuade me to marry again, which makes me feel worse.

MADAM. (Furious) The old rascal! He'll wish he'd never been born when I've done talking to him tonight.

PRECIOUS STREAM. Oh, no! Please don't quarrel with Father on *my* account. It will only increase my sin against filial piety.

MADAM. Very well, then. He has you to thank if I let him off. How are you feeling now?

PRECIOUS STREAM. You see I have already recovered at the sight of you.

MADAM. But this is not the place for convalescence. Now be reasonable, and come back with your mother, where you need not worry about anything, and will have plenty to eat and plenty to wear.

PRECIOUS STREAM. No, dear Mother—I'd rather starve here than go back.

MADAM. Nonsense! Now tell me, when did you last hear from your husband?

PRECIOUS STREAM. I have never heard from him since his departure. The official news declared that there was a general defeat. Not long ago when the troops of the Western Region retired, our search party returned with the report that my husband was amongst those who were killed.

MADAM. Oh, my dear, let us hope that he has escaped somehow and will return safe and sound.

PRECIOUS STREAM. Thank you, dear Mother. But I had hoped he would return victorious. To return as a deserter or an escaped prisoner would be worse than not to return at all.

MADAM. Oh, brave girl! I think the best way for you is to come back with me, and if your father tries to say anything against you he will have *me* to deal with.

PRECIOUS STREAM. *(Determined)* No! I am afraid you'll have to go back alone, dear Mother. And if Father refers to me, tell him to regard me as dead, or still better, regard me as never having been born.

MADAM. Don't be stupid. Don't mind your father. Don't worry about your husband. Come to your mother. The place where your mother is is the place for you; and the place where your mother goes is the place where you should go. Your mother will protect you. And when your mother dies you will be her chief mourner, won't you?

PRECIOUS STREAM. Of course, of course!

MADAM. And when your father dies, don't mourn for him, and don't weep for him at all.

PRECIOUS STREAM. *(Coaxing her)* No, no, I won't weep for him at all. It is you, and only you, whom I love and whom I will mourn and weep for. Do you feel satisfied now?

MADAM. Yes. But since you refuse to go with me, I will stay with you here instead.

PRECIOUS STREAM. *(Rises)* Oh, no! You can't stay here.

MADAM. I am determined.

PRECIOUS STREAM. *(Crosses down L.)* This will never do! *(The* SERVANTS, MAIDS *and* DRIVER *return from up* R. *and stop down* R.*)* This will never do.

MADAM. You can't force me to go.

PRECIOUS STREAM. I hear the servants coming. I

think you ought to go now, dear Mother. (PROPERTY MAN L. *moves stool.*)

MADAM. *(Rises)* No. My maids, bring in the silver and the rice and the clothes that you have brought with you.

MAIDS. Yes, Madam. *(They enter and ascend stairs.)*

MADAM. Give them to Lady Precious Stream.

MAIDS. Yes, Madam. *(They cross to L. of PRECIOUS STREAM.)*

MAIDS. These are for you, Lady Precious Stream.

MADAM. Put them down.

PRECIOUS STREAM. No, Mother. I won't take anything from the Wang family. (MAIDS *put down parcels. They are removed by* PROPERTY MAN L. MAIDS *return to positions down* R.)

MADAM. Nonsense! These are presents from me to you. They have nothing to do with the Wang family. Besides, when I am staying with you we shall need a little money to buy some extra food. You can't expect me to live on rice pudding all the time.

PRECIOUS STREAM. Dear Mother, you can't stay here with me.

MADAM. Can't I? You'll see. Attendants!

ATTENDANTS. *(Kneeling)* Yes, Madam?

MADAM. All of you may go home now, for I'm going to stay a few days here with Lady Precious Stream. *(She sits.)*

ATTENDANTS. *(Rising)* Yes, Madam.

PRECIOUS STREAM. Wait, please. What shall I do? What shall I do? *(Tapping her forehead)* Ah! I have it. Well, Mother, I have changed my mind. I agree to return with you rather than let you stay here with me.

MADAM. *(Rising)* That's a good girl. Attendants! Prepare the carriage for us. Lead the way, my darling. *(They commence to go out of cave.* ATTEND-

ANTS *cross to down* L. DRIVER *arranges carriage.*
PROPERTY MAN R. *removes chair.)*

PRECIOUS STREAM. Mind the steps, Mother. Oh,
Mother, I forgot something.

MADAM. What is it, my darling?

PRECIOUS STREAM. I forgot to put the silver, the
clothes and the rice in a safe place.

MADAM. They won't be lost if the cave door is
locked.

PRECIOUS STREAM. But the rats—they will eat the
rice and destroy the clothes. (BOTH *enter carriage.)*

MADAM. They are worth very little. I can afford
to get some more.

PRECIOUS STREAM. I can't allow anything from
my dear mother to be destroyed. I won't be a moment.

MADAM. Then be quick. (PROPERTY MAN L. *places
cushion after* PRECIOUS STREAM *has gone into cave.*
PRECIOUS STREAM *runs into the cave, bolts door and
falls on her knees* C.)

PRECIOUS STREAM. Mother, I am not going back
with you. And for my unfilial conduct I am kneeling
inside the cave.

MADAM. Oh, my obstinate darling, how could you?

PRECIOUS STREAM. Dear Mother, though I remain in the cave, my heart goes with you.

MADAM. *(To the* MAIDS*)* My maids, try to get
Lady Precious Stream to open the door and come
with me. (MAIDS *cross* L. *to* R. *of* PRECIOUS STREAM.
PROPERTY MAN L. *knocks on his box as* MAIDS *pretend to knock on cave door.)*

1ST MAID. *(Knocks at cave)* Lady Precious
Stream, will you please open the door and come
back with us?

PRECIOUS STREAM. No, dear maids. I sincerely
entreat you, instead of trying to persuade me to
come out, to try your best to make Madam, my
mother, depart as quickly as possible. The weather

is cold and the North wind is bitter. If you will do this favor for me, you will have the eternal gratitude of an unfilial daughter.

MAIDS. We will, we will! *(They move R. to above* MADAM.)

1ST MAID. Madam, Lady Precious Stream refuses to come out. She entreats you to return as soon as possible, for it is bitterly cold here.

2D MAID. If you will allow me to say a word, Madam, I think she is quite determined, and we had better go home ourselves, and come back some other time.

MADAM. *(Weeping)* Oh, my poor, darling daughter.

PRECIOUS STREAM. *(Weeping)* Oh, my poor, dear Mother.

1ST MAID. *(To the* SERVANTS) I think we had better start at once. (MAIDS *return to places behind* DRIVER.)

MADAM. Start! *(They go round stage once and exit up* L.)

PRECIOUS STREAM. *(Listens to them leave and comes out of cave to* C.) Oh, she has gone!

(MUSIC starts. As PRECIOUS STREAM *exits up* L. *MUSIC stops. STAGE LIGHTS fade. HOUSE LIGHTS on.)*

END OF ACT TWO

(NO CURTAIN)

(During the intermission the PROPERTY MEN *rearrange their property boxes, sweep stage, etc.)*

ACT THREE

(HOUSE LIGHTS out. GONG #1. Enter READER *from down* L. *SPOTLIGHT on* READER.*)*

READER. We are now coming to a strange land known as the Western Regions. It is believed that the customs here are exactly opposite those of China. For instance, the women wear long gowns whilst the men wear short coats and have their trousers showing. Their appearance, too, is unusual. They have red hair, green eyes, prominent noses and hairy hands. The stage represents the magnificent court of the King of the Western Regions. Probably they have very queer furniture and very strange decorations. Indeed we would be quite at a loss to prepare the properties of this scene had we not the advantage of leaving the audience to furnish them according to their imagination. Everything in this scene is strange. But the most strange thing of all is that His Majesty the King is no other than our old friend the gardener, Hsieh Ping-Kuei, whom we believed the enemy killed long ago, is still alive, and after his conquest of the Western Regions has proclaimed himself King. To our regret no records of this conquest exist and we regret even more having arrived a day too late to see his coronation. However, another great occasion is coming very soon. It has been arranged that a royal wedding is to take place tomorrow. The Queen Elect is a foreign Prin-

cess with whom our hero shares the laurels of his
victories. She is another clever woman who has suc-
ceeded in making our hero put a halter willingly
around his own neck. There is a general rumor to
the effect that there is a reluctance on his part to the
marriage, and the people wonder why such a beautiful maiden should not be snapped up with alacrity.
But we know that the cause is not due to this excellent lady whom we are going to meet soon, but to
His Majesty, who has some dark secret that he
dares not reveal. That is why we find that the first
gentleman of the kingdom is rather depressed in
this hour of what should be great happiness. He
seems to know that among the audience many are
doubtful of his identity so he introduces himself to
them once more. (READER *exits down* L.)

(GONG #2. STAGE LIGHTS up. PROPERTY MEN
enter L. *and* R. *GONG #3. MUSIC starts.
Enter* 1ST *and* 2D ATTENDANTS, *followed by*
HSIEH. ATTENDANTS *cross to down* R. *and down*
L. HSIEH *to down* C. *MUSIC stops.)*

HSIEH. *(Saluting)* By the help of the Royal Princess I have now the honor to be your humble servant
Hsieh Ping-Kuei, the King of the Western Regions.
I have been away from my home for eighteen years.
There are two things I desire perpetually; to return
to my wife, Precious Stream, and to avenge myself
on Wei, the Tiger General, who attempted to have
me murdered and nearly caused my death. When I
returned victorious, General Wei pretended to celebrate my triumph by giving a banquet in his camp,
and having made me quite intoxicated with strong
wine, tied me on to a horse and set it galloping
toward the enemy. (PROPERTY MAN L. *places table*
C. PROPERTY MAN R. *places chair* C. *above table.)*
Luckily I was rescued by the Princess, who released

me and helped me conquer all the Western Regions, from which she revolted for love of me. She wishes to marry me, an unusual proposal which I could not possibly refuse. Postponing it again and again I have at last been obliged to promise to marry her after my coronation. *(Crosses* c.; *sits)* Whilst everyone else in the kingdom seems to be rejoicing at the prospect of the coming wedding, I alone am troubled by it. (PROPERTY MAN R. *places chair down* R. *for* WILD GOOSE. WILD GOOSE *enters up* R.; *crosses down* R. *onto chair.)* I have been vainly trying to explain to her that I am already married, but I can't bear to break her heart. What shall I do? What *shall* I do?

WILD GOOSE. Hsieh Ping-Kuei's unfaithful! *(The* WILD GOOSE *continues to repeat this phrase over and over, sotto voce, until shot.)*

ATTENDANTS. We beg to report to your Majesty that a wild goose is flying over the palace, uttering strange sounds.

HSIEH. *(Rises; crosses down* L.C.*)* Show me where it is.

ATTENDANTS. *(Pointing)* There is the bird, Your Majesty.

HSIEH. This is strange. It seems to keep uttering that I'm unfaithful. This is indeed a bad omen. Attendants, bring me my bow and arrows.

ATTENDANTS. Yes, Your Majesty. (1ST ATTENDANT *gets bow from* PROPERTY MAN L. *and gives it to* HSIEH.)

HSIEH. I have never before heard a wild goose uttering sounds which seem to be like the words of a human being. With my bow and arrow I shoot it. There! *(He shoots.* WILD GOOSE *makes movements as though shot and exits up* R. 2D ATTENDANT *gets piece of cloth from* PROPERTY MAN R.*)*

2D ATTENDANT. I beg to report to Your Majesty that I found this piece of cloth on the bird.

HSIEH. *(Crossing to* C.*)* Give it to me.

2D ATTENDANT. *(Handing it to him)* Yes, Your Majesty.

HSIEH. *(After looking at cloth)* Ah! Attendants, retire for a moment, please. (ATTENDANTS *exit up* L. *and* R.) The words on the cloth, torn from her skirt, are written with her blood. They say, "Precious Stream presents her respects to her unfaithful husband, Hsieh Ping-Kuei, and begs to tell him that since his departure she has been suffering every hardship in the humble cave. If he returns immediately, they may meet each other once more, but if he delays for only a few days, they may never see each other again." Oh, my dear wife, my dear Precious Stream. I cannot stop the tears flowing from my eyes. Far, far away there is my home, my sweet home. My dear wife. I must get back in time to see you. Let me ponder and think of some plan. Ah! I have it! (ATTENDANTS *enter from up* R. *and* L. *to down* R. *and down* L.) I must do it. I must do it at any cost. Attendants!

ATTENDANTS. Yes, Your Majesty.

HSIEH. Request Her Highness, the Royal Princess, to come to court. *(He sits up* R.)

ATTENDANTS. Yes, your Majesty. *(Cross up* R. *and up* L. *and call off* R.) His Majesty requests the presence of Her Highness, the Royal Princess.

PRINCESS. *(Off* R.) To hear is to obey. *(MUSIC starts. Enter* FOUR MAIDS *up* R. 1ST *and* 2D *cross down* R. *and then go to down* L. 3D *and* 4TH *cross down* R. PRINCESS *follows to down* C. ATTENDANTS *return to places down* L. *and down* R. *MUSIC stops. To audience, saluting)* Your humble maid, the Royal Princess of the Western Regions, at your service. I have just returned from the parade grounds after reviewing my troops and have been told that His Majesty has commanded me to go to court. *(To* MAIDS*)* My maids, lead the way to the court.

MAIDS. *(Saluting)* Yes, Your Highness. *(The*

MAIDS *cross to* C. *and then go up* L. *and make a large circle around the stage, returning to their original positions. The* PRINCESS *follows them but stops at* R. *of table.)*

PRINCESS. *(To* HSIEH, *saluting)* Your humble maid, the Royal Princess of the Western Regions, offers her respects to Your Majesty.

HSIEH. Don't stand on ceremony.

*(*PROPERTY MAN L. *places chair at* L. *of table.)*

PRINCESS. *(Crossing below table to chair* L.*)* Thank you.

HSIEH. You are at liberty to sit down. (MAIDS *cross directly to up* L.C. *and up* R.C., *standing above chairs.)*

PRINCESS. *(Sitting)* Thank you. May I know what important affair of state Your Majesty wishes to discuss with me?

HSIEH. There is no affair of state I wish to trouble you with. As you have been having a very hard time recently in reviewing all these troops, I have prepared a banquet in your honor, and I would be glad if you would consent to have a hearty carousal with me.

PRINCESS. *(Highly pleased)* This would indeed be a great honor. Allow me to serve Your Majesty with wine.

HSIEH. *(Signals* ATTENDANT R.*)* Oh, no, I couldn't possibly trouble you. Attendants! Prepare wine for me.

ATTENDANTS. Yes, Your Majesty.

HSIEH. *(To* PRINCESS*)* Let me have the pleasure of serving you. (1ST ATTENDANT *gets tray with wine jug and two glasses from* PROPERTY MAN R.; *puts them on table, then back to his place.* HSIEH *immediately pours out wine; hands glass to* PRINCESS. *She drinks.)* Although I am very happy in drinking with you, the thought of our being attacked by the neighboring states constantly troubles me.

PRINCESS. I beg Your Majesty not to worry about the invasion of other states, for I myself am able to cope with any invasion of the enemy regardless of the numbers.

HSIEH. Regardless of number?

PRINCESS. Yes! But of course we entirely depend upon your blessing, without which there is no chance of victory.

HSIEH. Oh, no, you are the invincible, Princess.

PRINCESS. Thank you. To Your Majesty's health! *(She finds that her cup is empty.)* More wine to Your Majesty!

HSIEH. How full of life and charm you are! *(Pours more wine)* Do not hesitate to refresh yourself thoroughly. You have had a hard time reviewing the troops, and a good bumper of wine will greatly benefit you.

PRINCESS. *(Pleased)* Oh, thanks, Your Majesty! But I can't drink as much as I could formerly.

HSIEH. How much could you drink formerly?

PRINCESS. A hundred cups at least!

HSIEH. And now?

PRINCESS. *(Smiling)* Only fifty cups, *(Strikes two cups together)* multiplied by two.

HSIEH. *(Laughing)* Ha, ha! Just the same! One hundred cups! *(To* ATTENDANTS*)* Attendants! Serve the wine in large cups.

ATTENDANTS. Yes, Your Majesty.

(MUSIC starts. ATTENDANT L. *removes tray and glasses from table, giving them to* PROPERTY MAN L. ATTENDANT R. *gets tray and two goblets and jug from* PROPERTY MAN R.; *places them on table, then back to their places.* HSIEH *pours out and gives* PRINCESS *goblet of wine. She drinks it; hands it to* MAID, *who passes it*

along to the MAID R., *who places it on table.*
HSIEH *repeats business of goblet passed round,
replaced on table.* HSIEH *then gives the* PRIN-
CESS *the jug, who sways in her seat and gradu-
ally sinks with head on table. MUSIC stops.)*

MAIDS. *(Look first at* PRINCESS, *then at each
other, then speak to audience)* Her Highness is intoxicated.

HSIEH. *(Raising her head)* So she is. *(Rises)* She
has fallen into my trap. (PROPERTY MAN L. *puts flag
in* PRINCESS's *belt.* HSIEH *moves to* R. *of* PRINCESS;
takes flag from her belt, then down to C. *to audience)*
Now I have done it. With this little flag I can go
where I like and get away from the Western Regions,
but I shall have to leave without bidding her good-
bye. (PROPERTY MAN R. *puts pen and paper on
table; removes goblets and jug.* HSIEH *sits at table)*
I will write a letter to her. I can't bear to say good-
bye to her. *(Reading as he writes)* "I am going to
the frontier to review the troops there. If you still
love me, follow me with all your troops to the third
pass; if you don't love me, stay where you are and
don't think of me." *(He rises)* Men of the Western
Region, saddle my horse!

ATTENDANTS. Yes, Your Majesty. (2D ATTEN-
DANT *gets whip from* PROPERTY MAN R.; *holds it
for* HSIEH, *who takes it.* HSIEH *leaps on his horse
and gallops off up* L.)

MAIDS. *(Step forward, waving hands)* Your Highness! Your Highness! (MAIDS *return to places up
stage.)*

PRINCESS. *(Waking up)* The wine has affected me
a little. Where is His Majesty? *(Looks under table.)*

1ST ATTENDANT. His Majesty has gone to the frontier to review the troops there, Your Highness.

PRINCESS. Did he leave any orders for me?

2D ATTENDANT. *(Picks up letter from table;*

hands it to her) His Majesty's left this letter for Your Highness.

Pʀɪɴᴄᴇss. *(Takes letter. Rising)* Let me read it. What does he mean? What *does* he mean? *(Pacing stage, tapping forehead)* Ah, I see! His Majesty has gone back to China. He wants me to follow him with all the troops to China. Attendants! *(Turns back to audience.)*

Aᴛᴛᴇɴᴅᴀɴᴛs. Yes, Your Highness.

Pʀɪɴᴄᴇss. Order my two aides-de-camp, Ma Ta and Kiang Hai, to await my further orders before the palace gates with all my troops.

Aᴛᴛᴇɴᴅᴀɴᴛs. Yes, Your Highness. (Pʀᴏᴘᴇʀᴛʏ Mᴀɴ ʟ. *removes chair* Pʀɪɴᴄᴇss *has used.* Pʀᴏᴘᴇʀᴛʏ Mᴀɴ ʀ. *moves armchair.* Pʀᴏᴘᴇʀᴛʏ Mᴀɴ ʟ. *clears table to up stage* ʟ. Aᴛᴛᴇɴᴅᴀɴᴛs *cross up* ʟ. *and up* ʀ., *turn* ʀ. *and call)* Her Highness orders her two aides-de-camp, Ma Ta and Kiang Hai, to await her further orders before the palace gates with all her troops.

Mᴀ Tᴀ *and* Kɪᴀɴɢ Hᴀɪ. *(Off stage)* To hear is to obey. (Aᴛᴛᴇɴᴅᴀɴᴛs *return to places down* ʟ. *and down* ʀ.)

Pʀɪɴᴄᴇss. *(Facing audience)* How unreasonable His Majesty is. He ought not to have gone away without bidding me goodbye. I will overtake him with my troops and ask him what is the reason. (Pʀɪɴᴄᴇss, *facing her* Mᴀɪᴅs, *gestures them to precede her.* Mᴀɪᴅs *salute; face* ʟ.; *march off up* ʟ., *followed by* Aᴛᴛᴇɴᴅᴀɴᴛs *and* Pʀɪɴᴄᴇss.)

(Enter Mᴀ Tᴀ *and* Kɪᴀɴɢ Hᴀɪ *up* ʀ., *getting spears from* Pʀᴏᴘᴇʀᴛʏ Mᴀɴ ʀ., *down stage to* ᴄ., *to audience.)*

Mᴀ Tᴀ. Our home is far, far in the Northwest.

Kɪᴀɴɢ Hᴀɪ. We are somewhat tongue-tied.

Mᴀ Tᴀ. Beef and mutton are what we like best.

KIANG HAI. Big camels are what we ride.

MA TA. *(Saluting)* I am Ma Ta, at your service.

KIANG HAI. I am Kiang Hai, your humble servant.

MA TA. Glad to see you.

KIANG HAI. How goes it?

MA TA *and* KIANG HAI. We are here waiting for orders from Her Highness, the Royal Princess. *(They take one step back; turn; face each other; two steps back.)*

(Enter MAIDS up L., two down R., two L., followed by PRINCESS, who comes C. MAIDS get spears and PRINCESS's whip from PROPERTY MAN R.)

PRINCESS. Oh, unfaithful Hsieh Ping-Kuei, I will overtake you and sue you for breach of promise.

MA TA *and* KIANG HAI. *(Saluting)* Our respects to you, Your Highness.

PRINCESS. Don't stand on ceremony. Are the troops ready?

MA TA *and* KIANG HAI. Yes, Your Highness. We are waiting for your orders.

PRINCESS. Order them to march to the first pass.

MA TA *and* KIANG HAI. *(Calling)* To the first pass.

(MUSIC starts. MAIDS L. turn upstage; start marching, followed by MAIDS R. They exit up L., followed by MA TA, KIANG HAI and PRINCESS. Pass brought on up R. by 1ST and 2D SOLDIERS. WARDEN comes on R.; stands on chair behind it. MUSIC stops.)

WARDEN. By the order of Her Highness, the Royal Princess of the Western Regions, I am the Warden of the first pass.

HSIEH. *(Enters up* R.; *down to* L.) Hey! Open the pass for me!

WARDEN. Where do you come from and what is your business?

HSIEH. By the orders of Her Highness, the Royal Princess, I have business of State to transact beyond the pass.

WARDEN. Have you the yellow flag from Her Highness—

HSIEH. Yes—here it is.

WARDEN. Soldiers, open the pass for him.

(MUSIC starts. HSIEH *up stage, through the pass and off* L. MAIDS *enter up* R.; *march to* L.; *make line up and down stage,* MA TA *and* KIANG HAI *following them. A division is left between the* FOUR MAIDS. PRINCESS *enters up* R.; *across to* L.; *comes to* L.C. *through the division between* MAIDS. *MUSIC stops.)*

WARDEN. The Warden of the first pass pays his respects to you, Your Highness.

PRINCESS. Don't stand on ceremony. I want to ask you, has His Majesty the King passed here?

WARDEN. *(Trembling)* There was a man who passed through, but I don't know if it was His Majesty the King.

PRINCESS. Don't you even know your King? You are under arrest! To the second pass.

(MUSIC starts. 1ST MAID *starts, followed by other* MAIDS, MA TA *and* KIANG HAI. *They march in front of* PRINCESS. *She follows them.* ALL *go through pass and exit up* L. *Pass is moved to* C. *stage.* WARDEN *changes beard. MUSIC stops.)*

WARDEN. By order of her Royal Highness, the

Princess of the Western Regions, I am the Warden of the second pass.

HSIEH. *(Enters up* R.; *to down* L.) Hey! Open the pass for me!

WARDEN. Where do you come from and what is your business?

HSIEH. By the order of her Highness, the Royal Princess, I have business of state to transact beyond the pass.

WARDEN. Have you the yellow flag from Her Highness?

HSIEH. Yes, here it is.

WARDEN. Soldiers, open the pass for him. *(MUSIC starts.* HSIEH *goes through the pass and off up* L. MAIDS *march in up* R. *as before; below pass to* L., *leaving division between them for* PRINCESS. PRINCESS *enters up* R. *through the division to* L.C. *MUSIC stops.)* The Warden of the second pass presents his respects to Your Highness.

PRINCESS. Don't stand on ceremony. I want to ask you. Has His Majesty, the King, passed here?

WARDEN. A man did pass here, but—

PRINCESS. Excellent service you're rendering me. Report yourself for court martial tomorrow morning. To the third pass!

(MUSIC starts. MAIDS, MA TA, KIANG HAI *and* PRINCESS *march through pass and exit up* L. *as before.* WARDEN *joins in the march after* MAIDS *and before* MA TA *and exits with them. Pass is moved to* L. MU *enters and stands on chair behind pass. MUSIC stops.)*

MU. I am well known for my white helmet, white armor, and white banners. I also have a white moustache, white beard, and white eyebrows. After I have drunk plenty of white wine I will show you the whites of my eyes! I am old Mu, the White General, at your service. By order of His Imperial Majesty, the Emperor, I am the Warden of the third pass.

HSIEH. *(Enters up* R.; *down to* C. *To audience)* Wait! This is now the frontier of my motherland. The third pass is the boundary. The man in the tower seems to be old General Mu. Let me call him by name. *(Crosses up to pass)* My respects to you, Old General Mu.

MU. Thank you. Thank you. Who are you to call me by name?

HSIEH. I am Captain Hsieh Ping-Kuei coming back from the Western Regions to report myself at headquarters.

MU. The pass is haunted! The pass is haunted! (MU *gets down behind the pass.* SOLDIERS *shake the pass.)* You were killed in the Western Regions. So this is your spirit which comes back to haunt me.

HSIEH. No, I was not killed. My enemy planned my death and thinks I am dead but I am still alive.

MU. *(Poking head through pass)* Is that so? I can hardly believe it.

MAIDS. *(Off)* Houp-hey!

HSIEH. There are troops in pursuit of me. Open the pass and let me in.

MU. All right. Open the pass for him, soldiers.

(MUSIC starts. HSIEH *goes through pass and exits up* L. MAIDS *enter up* R., *followed by* MA TA *and* KIANG HAI. *They form a line as before. The* PRINCESS *goes between them to* C. ALL *are very tired. MUSIC stops.)*

MA TA *and* KIANG HAI. We beg to report to Your Highness that we have now arrived at the third pass, which belongs to China.

PRINCESS. *(Crossing* R.*)* So we have! Go and ask them to let us pass through.

MA TA *and* KIANG HAI. *(Crossing* L.*)* Yes, Your Highness.

PRINCESS. *(Turning* L.*)* One moment. Come back!

MA TA *and* KIANG HAI. *(Turning* R.*)* Yes, Your Highness.

PRINCESS. As we have come to the territory of another country we must be more polite in our speech.

MA TA *and* KIANG HAI. Yes, Your Highness. *(They face* MU.*)*

MA TA. Hey! My old man!

MU. Old moon? Can't see the old moon until midnight.

KIANG HAI. My master!

MU. Mustard! Go to the grocery for it.

MA TA. My Lord!

MU. He is in Heaven.

KIANG HAI. My Emperor!

MU. You are empty?—This is not an eating house. What are you two doing here? You are too ugly to be called human beings, and certainly too ordinary to be called devils. Go back and get someone more presentable to talk to me. *(They turn to* PRINCESS.*)*

MA TA *and* KIANG HAI. He requests the presence of Your Highness.

PRINCESS. All right. I'll go. *(She goes to upper corner of the pass.* MA TA *and* KIANG HAI *return to their places in line.)* My respects to you, old grandfather in the tower.

MU. Thank you, and mine to the little grandmother beneath it. What is your business here?

PRINCESS. May I ask you, has His Majesty, the King of our country, Captain Hsieh Ping-Kuei of your country, passed through this way?

MU. His Majesty the King of your country has not passed but Captain Hsieh Ping-Kuei of our country has passed.

PRINCESS. But he is no other than the King of

our country. If he has passed here and is with you there, I entreat you to ask him to appear on the wall of the pass so that we may say a few words to each other. Then I will withdraw with my forces, and I promise you there will be no trouble and no damage. Do you think this can be done, my old General?

MU. You bewitching little minx! Captain Hsieh Ping-Kuei of our country used to be a robust young giant, and now, after eighteen years adventure in your country, he comes back the wreck of a man. How can I allow him to see you again, you little minx?

PRINCESS. *(Furious)* What impudence! *(Crosses R.)* Ma Ta and Kiang Hai!

MA TA *and* KIANG HAI. Yes, Your Highness!

PRINCESS. Attack the pass!

ALL. Houp-Hey! ! (ALL *take one step forward as if to attack pass with spears.)*

MU. Wait a moment! Wait a moment! The pass is made of cloth; it will be damaged if you don't take care. (PRINCESS *motions them to stand at ease again.)* If you withdraw for a short distance, I will ask Captain Hsieh Ping-Kuei to come out and speak to you. After all, I am not his guardian, and I don't care what company he keeps.

PRINCESS. *(Crosses to pass)* You must play fair.

MU. Of course! Fair play for a fair lady.

PRINCESS. The troops are ordered to withdraw to a short distance. *(They ALL do a Left turn.)*

MA TA *and* KIANG HAI. Yes, Your Highness. *(They march off up* R., MAIDS *going off first.)*

MU. Captain Hsieh! Captain Hsieh!

HSIEH. *(Appearing from up* L.) May I congratulate you on your victory?

MU. Congratulate the lady, my enemy! The victory belongs to her. You are requested to go up to the tower; she wants to speak to you. *(Gets down from chair.)*

HSIEH. Thank you for your trouble. (MU *exits up* L.) I see the Princess coming alone.

PRINCESS. *(Appearing again)* I see the unfaithful one standing alone. *(To* HSIEH*)* What have I done to deserve this? Why did you desert me?

HSIEH. I will tell you everything now. The other day a wild goose brought a letter from Lady Precious Stream.

PRINCESS. What! Who is this Lady Precious Stream?

HSIEH. She is my wife.

PRINCESS. *(Appalled)* What—your wife! So you are already married! You are going back to her now?

HSIEH. Yes.

PRINCESS. Oh, you have been deceiving me all these years.

HSIEH. *(Protesting)* No. You wrong me there. I was desperately in love with you all the time, and I am still.

PRINCESS. Then why do you forsake me?

HSIEH. Because I am in honor bound to the other.

PRINCESS. But you ought to have told me this before.

HSIEH. I loved you too much to hurt your feelings.

PRINCESS. To deceive me and then desert me is most heartless. *(Crosses down* R.*)* I will never speak to you again. I hate you! I hate you!

HSIEH. *(Hurt)* Please don't! I *still* love you. Will you be a sister to me and go to China with me?

PRINCESS. Never. Never! I don't want to be near you now.

HSIEH. But I want to be near you. That's why I asked you to follow me.

PRINCESS. Yes, but at a safe distance.

HSIEH. Don't say that. I would gladly marry you if I could. Now, will you not be my sister and come with me?

PRINCESS. Never!

HSIEH. Then I must bid you farewell forever, because I may never see you again.

PRINCESS. I don't want to see you again.

HSIEH. I have many enemies in China, and without your military protection I shall probably be murdered by them very soon.

PRINCESS. Oh, I never thought of that. Yes, your General Wei will try to murder you. I must go with you to protect you, even if I hate you. *(Crosses few steps L.)*

HSIEH. No! I can't accept your protection if you still hate me.

PRINCESS. *(Crosses a step L.)* Well, I won't hate you.

HSIEH. And will be my sister?

PRINCESS. *(Crosses a step L.)* No! At most your cousin.

HSIEH. No! Sister.

PRINCESS. *(Crosses a step L.)* Let us say first cousin?

HSIEH. No! Sister.

PRINCESS. *(Crosses to C.)* All right. Come down at once.

HSIEH. No! In Lady Precious Stream's letter she said she is in great danger, so I must hurry on. Order your troops to be encamped near the pass and await a message from me. Goodbye till then. (HSIEH *exits up L., followed by* SOLDIERS *carrying pass.)*

PRINCESS. Goodbye. *(Calling off R.)* Ma Ta and Kiang Hai!

MA TA *and* KIANG HAI. *(Off R.)* Yes, Your Highness.

PRINCESS. Order the troops to be encamped here.

MA TA *and* KIANG HAI. Yes, Your Highness.

(MUSIC starts. MAIDS *enter up R., followed by* MA TA *and* KIANG HAI. *They cross and exit up L.,*

followed by the PRINCESS. *LIGHTS dim. MU-*
SIC stops. LIGHTS up.)

HSIEH. Look out! A horse is coming! *(Enters up*
R. *Crosses to down* C.*)* When one is anxious to get
home one travels both in daytime and by starlight.
Bidding goodbye to the Princess not long ago, I have
now arrived at the little hill not far from my own
door. *(He dismounts to* R.*; gives whip to* PROPERTY
MAN R.*)* Let me tie my horse under the shadow of
a willow tree. *(To audience.* PRECIOUS STREAM *en-*
ters up L.*; gets basket from* PROPERTY MAN L. *Dur-*
ing the following speech she crosses down L.*, then*
crosses stage to down R.*)* There is someone coming.
She looks rather like my wife, but, I must be careful to avoid being guilty of taking another man's
wife as my own. Now that I have arrived at my
home, I must be very polite. *(Crosses to down* L.*;*
faces R.*)* My respects to you, Madam. May I have
a word with you?
PRECIOUS STREAM. *(Faces* L.*; curtseys)* And mine
to you. Have you lost your way, sir?
HSIEH. *(Crossing to down* L.C.*)* No one could be
lost in such a place as this. I want to find someone.
PRECIOUS STREAM. *(Crossing to down* R.C.*)* Only
famous people are known to me.
HSIEH. She whom I seek is a very famous person. She is the daughter of the Prime Minister Wang
and the wife of Hsieh Ping-Kuei. Lady Precious
Stream she is by name.
PRECIOUS STREAM. May I ask why you are in-
quiring for her?
HSIEH. I have been serving in the same company
as her husband, who has entrusted me with a letter
for her.
PRECIOUS STREAM. Let me have the letter.
HSIEH. Oh, no, Madam. Hsieh Ping-Kuei said
this letter should be delivered in person—by me.

PRECIOUS STREAM. Please excuse me a moment.

HSIEH. Certainly. *(He crosses up* L. *to* PROPERTY MAN *and gets tea.)*

PRECIOUS STREAM. *(Crosses to audience)* I should like to confess and get that letter at once, but I am in such rags that I am ashamed to do so, and if I don't he will certainly not give me that letter. Oh, how cruel that for eighteen long years' separation we have never met and have not been able to correspond. What shall I do? *(Tapping forehead)* Ah! I have it. *(Turns to* HSIEH, *who has come back down* L.C.*)* Well, sir, do you understand riddles?

HSIEH. A little.

PRECIOUS STREAM. Do you want to see Precious Stream?

HSIEH. Yes.

PRECIOUS STREAM. Now, if you look far—

HSIEH. —she is a thousand miles away.

PRECIOUS STREAM. Yes, and if you look near—

HSIEH. —she is before me. Am I speaking to Mrs. Hsieh, the famous daughter of the Prime Minister Wang?

PRECIOUS STREAM. Oh, no, not the famous, but only the humble wife of Hsieh Ping-Kuei.

HSIEH. *(Bowing)* My respects to you.

PRECIOUS STREAM. *(Curtseying)* You have already paid your respects.

HSIEH. Over-politeness does no harm.

PRECIOUS STREAM. Well said. Now my husband's letter, please.

HSIEH. One moment. Will you excuse me a minute?

PRECIOUS STREAM. Certainly. *(Crosses up* R. *to get tea from* PROPERTY MAN.*)*

HSIEH. *(Crosses to audience)* Wait a moment! I was married to her for only a month, and I have been absent from home for eighteen years. I don't know what kind of a woman she really is. Let me try to flirt with her. If she proves to be a good and virtuous woman, I'll tell her who I am and we'll be happily reunited. But if she proves to be a woman of easy virtue, I'll disown her and go back to the Royal Princess of the Western Regions. *(Crosses to L.C. PRECIOUS STREAM crosses to R.C.)* Ah! Where on earth is that letter?

PRECIOUS STREAM. Where is it?

HSIEH. It is lost, Madam.

PRECIOUS STREAM. Don't you know that a letter from one who loves you is worth all the money in the world? You should remember our sage said: "I examine myself three times every day to see whether I have done truly and loyally my best to my friend." And you have lost the letter of your friend. I am heartbroken.

HSIEH. Don't take it so seriously, Madam. If you're so anxious about that letter, I'll tell you something I remember that is in it.

PRECIOUS STREAM. Please tell me what you do remember.

HSIEH. Listen carefully. "On the mid-Autumn night, under the bright moonlight, Hsieh Ping-Kuei presents his compliments to his dear wife—"

PRECIOUS STREAM. And mine to him. How has he been lately?

HSIEH. Very well.

PRECIOUS STREAM. Safe and sound?

HSIEH. Safe and sound.

PRECIOUS STREAM. How about his meals?

HSIEH. They were badly cooked by the soldiers.

PRECIOUS STREAM. How about his clothes?

HSIEH. He has had to wash and mend them himself. "—and begs to tell her that he has been very unfortunate lately. He has suffered severe torture—"

PRECIOUS STREAM. Oh, torture! He was beaten?

HSIEH. Yes, Madam, beaten.

PRECIOUS STREAM. How many strokes did he receive?

HSIEH. Forty strokes in all.

PRECIOUS STREAM. Oh, my poor husband.

HSIEH. Don't cry, Madam. There are still worse things coming. "The other day a horse under his care was lost."

PRECIOUS STREAM. Was it a Government horse or a privately owned one?

HSIEH. How can there be any privately owned horses in a camp? Of course it was a Government one.

PRECIOUS STREAM. That being so I suppose he will have to pay for it.

HSIEH. How can he avoid paying for it?

PRECIOUS STREAM. But where can he find the money to pay for it?

HSIEH. He is sure to be able to find the money in some way or other. "And because of having to pay for the horse, he has had to borrow ten pieces of silver—" Borrowed from me! *(Moves nearer her.)*

PRECIOUS STREAM. Stop! Allow me to ask you, what is your rank? *(Forces him* L. *one step.)*

HSIEH. I am a Captain.

PRECIOUS STREAM. *(Another step* L.*)* And my husband, Hsieh Ping-Kuei?

HSIEH. Also a Captain.

PRECIOUS STREAM. *(Two steps* L.*)* If you're both Captains, you should get the same amount of pay. Then how could you be able to lend him money whilst he had none?

HSIEH. Oh, there is a reason, Madam! My eldest brother, Hsieh Ping-Kuei, is a born spendthrift who squanders all his pay, whilst I, having been born in a humble family, have been accustomed to save all I get. In this way I was able to lend him the money to pay for the horse—

PRECIOUS STREAM. That is not true. My husband

was also born in a humble family, and he wouldn't know how to spend his money even if he tried. *(Crosses down R.C.)*

HSIEH. *(Laughing)* Ha, ha!

PRECIOUS STREAM. *(To audience)* Oh, dear, he is laughing at me!

HSIEH. *(Crosses to* PRECIOUS STREAM*)* The other day I went to his camp to demand the money and he said that he has a wife at home called Lady Precious Stream of the Wang family.

PRECIOUS STREAM. *(Furious, forces* HSIEH *one step L.)* Stop! Let me ask you, has Precious Stream ever owed you anything formerly?

HSIEH. No, nothing.

PRECIOUS STREAM. *(Another step L.)* Has she borrowed anything from you recently?

HSIEH. No, nothing.

PRECIOUS STREAM. *(One more step L.)* Why should her name be mentioned?

HSIEH. *(Forces* PRECIOUS STREAM *one step R.)* Well, let me ask you now. As our old proverb says, "Father's debts—"

PRECIOUS STREAM. "—the son pays."

HSIEH. *(Another step R.)* And the husband's debts?

PRECIOUS STREAM. The wife—the wife doesn't care a fig for them. *(Turns her back on him.)*

HSIEH. Well said. But the wife has to pay for them in some other way. Having no ready money, my eldest brother Hsieh agreed to sell his wife, and you know, Madam, he did not need to be afraid of there being no bidders, so a bargain was immediately made with a certain officer.

PRECIOUS STREAM. And who is this certain officer?

HSIEH. Eh—eh— *(With a smile)* Do you understand riddles, Madam?

PRECIOUS STREAM. Have you the audacity to say that it is you?

HSIEH. Eh—I haven't the audacity, but I have the proof.

PRECIOUS STREAM. What is your proof?

HSIEH. In the form of a marriage contract.

PRECIOUS STREAM. *(To audience)* Oh, cruel! No, I can't believe it. *(To* HSIEH *)* Who are the witnesses to the contract?

HSIEH. *(Tapping forehead and crossing* L.*)* They are—they are—Su, the Dragon General; Wei, the Tiger General; and Wang Yun, the Prime Minister.

PRECIOUS STREAM. Nonsense! I won't believe it, because they are all my near relatives and they would certainly not allow my husband to sell me. *(PRECIOUS STREAM doesn't look at* HSIEH. HSIEH *crosses up* L. *and hides.)* Though I am poor, my father is rich. Let me make out how much the capital and interest amount to now and I will send the money to you. I won't detain you now. Goodbye, and wait for the money in the Western Regions. *(PRECIOUS STREAM crosses up* R. *to be stopped by* HSIEH, *who has crossed from up* L.*)*

HSIEH. *(Forcing her down* C.*)* No, no! It took me forty-eight days to travel from the Western Regions to here, and I have come here specially, not for the money but for the beauty.

PRECIOUS STREAM. If you go on uttering nonsense and insulting me, I'll call for help and have you arrested.

HSIEH. But you are as good as my wife.

PRECIOUS STREAM. Oh, what impudence!

HSIEH. *(Rises on toes with arms outspread and lunges at her)* I am going to capture you and carry you off to the Western Regions.

PRECIOUS STREAM. *(Retreating to down* L.—*to audience)* Oh, I'm frightened. The man is a beast! What shall I do? There is no help within reach. Let

me think! *(Taps forehead)* Ah! I have it. I'll throw
dust in his eyes. *(To imaginary person off* R.*)* Hello,
sir! *(To* HSIEH*)* Someone is coming over there.

HSIEH. *(Turning* R. PRECIOUS STREAM *stoops to
pick up dust.)* Where? *(Turns back to* PRECIOUS
STREAM.*)*

PRECIOUS STREAM. *(Rising and pretending to
throw dust)* Goodbye! *(She crosses up* L. *and around
the stage.)*

HSIEH. *(Wiping eyes and crossing down* R.*)* Ah,
ha! A virtuous woman indeed! No use flirting with
her. *(Gets whip from* PROPERTY MAN*)* It's not very
far, so I will not ride but walk to my cave to meet
her. *(Crosses to* L. *and follows* PRECIOUS STREAM.*)*

PRECIOUS STREAM. It's too bad. He's following me.

HSIEH. I am your husband, Hsieh Ping-Kuei.
*(*PRECIOUS STREAM *enters cave; bolts door.* PROPER-
TY MAN L. *places chair with back to audience at down*
C. *beside her.* HSIEH *stops at* L.C.*)*

PRECIOUS STREAM. Let me shut the door and bolt
it.

HSIEH. Open the door! You are shutting out your
own husband.

PRECIOUS STREAM. You said but a short time ago
that you were an officer of the same regiment as my
husband, and now you are my husband. You are out
of your senses.

HSIEH. *(Kneels down to talk through door.* PREC-
IOUS STREAM *is kneeling inside door.)* Oh, no! Don't
you remember, you told me to be present on the second of February when I received the embroidered
ball? We were driven out by your father and lived
in this cave. Then I shot and killed the man-devour-
ing tiger and was made a Captain joining the Western Punitive Expedition? I came back to tell you
the news. I couldn't bear to leave you. Time was
pressing, and I had to cut the reins of my horse which

you held tightly in your hands. Then we parted and that was eighteen years ago.

PRECIOUS STREAM. Did you receive my letter?

HSIEH. Oh, yes. That is why I hurried home.

PRECIOUS STREAM. *(Rises and peeks out)* Let me look at— *(Closes door again)* No. How can you be my husband with such a strange beard? My husband is a very handsome young man.

HSIEH. Thank you, my third Sister. But you ought to say he used to be a handsome young man. Take yourself, for instance, my dear third Sister; you're quite different from the young girl who threw the ball from the pavilion. Consult a looking-glass and tell me what you think.

PRECIOUS STREAM. Don't you know there is no looking-glass in the humble cave?

HSIEH. Oh, I forgot! Look into a basin of water as you always did formerly.

PRECIOUS STREAM. *(Crossing R.)* It is a long time now since I looked into a basin of water, not caring how I looked. *(Kneels)* Oh, horrible! I couldn't call myself Precious Stream now. *(Rises.)*

HSIEH. Now open the door and let me in.

PRECIOUS STREAM. *(Opens door and puts out hand)* Show me the letter first.

HSIEH. *(Hands letter to her)* Here is the letter.

PRECIOUS STREAM. *(Closes door; crosses R.)* Yes, this is the letter. Oh, my heavens!

HSIEH. Then why do you close the door again?

PRECIOUS STREAM. *(Kneeling)* I will open the door only on one condition.

HSIEH. What is your condition, please?

PRECIOUS STREAM. A very simple one. I only want you to go backwards one step.

HSIEH. *(He takes one step towards down stage)* All right, I have done so.

PRECIOUS STREAM. Another step, please.

HSIEH. *(Doing so)* All right. Now open the door.

PRECIOUS STREAM. One step more, please.

HSIEH. *(His foot dangling beyond the proscenium)* No, I can't! I have come to the end of things.

PRECIOUS STREAM. If you had not come to the end of things, I'm sure you would never have come back to me. And after you had deserted me for eighteeen years, your insulted me the moment you met me. What is there to live for? I'd rather die than take back such a husband.

HSIEH. Please don't say that. I entreat you to forgive me.

PRECIOUS STREAM. No.

HSIEH. I entreat you on my knees. *(He drops on R. knee)* Look. I am paying you my highest respects in the presence of hundreds.

PRECIOUS STREAM. *(Peeping through door)* No, I won't look at you. How about your other knee? I thought you said you were on your knees.

HSIEH. Oh, I beg your pardon. *(Slaps left knee and puts it down.)*

PRECIOUS STREAM. Ah, that's better. *(Rises; opens door by pulling chair which is removed by* PROPERTY MAN L.*)* Come in, my dear.

HSIEH. *(Rising and entering)* Thank you, my dear. *(He circles stage* L., *climbing the stairs, followed by* PRECIOUS STREAM.*)*

PRECIOUS STREAM. To what rank have you been promoted after all these years? (PROPERTY MAN L. *places chair up* C. *and stool to its* L.)

HSIEH. Eh? When your husband has returned from thousands of miles away, the first question you put to him is not about his health, nor his requiring food and drink, but about his rank. What is rank compared to food and drink? *(He sits in chair.)*

PRECIOUS STREAM. *(Sits on stool)* I haven't been very frequently in touch with food and drink during these eighteen years, so I am liable to forget them.

HSIEH. What do you mean? Do you mean to tell

me that you haven't had enough to eat and drink during my absence? I remember having made a handsome provision for you just before my departure.

PRECIOUS STREAM. What was it?

HSIEH. Ten hundredweight of firewood and five hundredweight of rice.

PRECIOUS STREAM. Ten hundredweight of firewood and five hundredweight of rice? Even presuming they had everlasting qualities, how could they possibly outlast the wear and tear of all these eighteen years?

HSIEH. Granted. But you ought to have gone to your father and brother-in-law Wei for additional supplies.

PRECIOUS STREAM. They said that your pay had ceased and offered to make me a loan, which I refused.

HSIEH. *(Rising)* Splendid! Goodbye!

PRECIOUS STREAM. *(Rising)* Where are you going?

HSIEH. To His Excellency, the Prime Minister's house.

PRECIOUS STREAM. *(Crossing to R. of HSIEH)* Don't go. My father is not very well.

HSIEH. What is the matter with him? (PROPERTY MAN *removes chair and stool.)*

PRECIOUS STREAM. The common sickness of great men who don't like to see their poor relatives.

HSIEH. It doesn't matter. I haven't that kind of sickness, and I will condescend to see him.

PRECIOUS STREAM. What are you talking about? *You* condescend to see His Excellency, the Prime Minister?

HSIEH. Yes, we have to sometimes.

PRECIOUS STREAM. What do you mean? The King is the only man in the world he would serve.

HSIEH. But I have not said that I am not a King.

PRECIOUS STREAM. *You* a king?

HSIEH. Yes—only the King of the Western Regions.

PRECIOUS STREAM. Only the King of the Western Regions! *(To audience)* This seems incredible. *(To HSIEH)* What proof have you?

HSIEH. What proof do you want?

PRECIOUS STREAM. Show me your royal seal.

HSIEH. Nonsense! Whoever heard of anyone having asked a King to prove himself a King by showing his royal seal?

PRECIOUS STREAM. I have never seen a royal seal, and I want very much to see one. Show it to me.

HSIEH. All right. If I have the royal seal—

PRECIOUS STREAM. Show it to me and I will believe you are a King.

HSIEH. And if I haven't the royal seal—

PRECIOUS STREAM. Then seal your lips so that you will utter no more nonsense.

HSIEH. Do you really want to see the royal seal?

PRECIOUS STREAM. Very much.

HSIEH. *(Paces L. a few steps)* Then let me adjust my hat and dust my jacket. (PROPERTY MAN L. *hands him seal.)* Here is the seal of the King of the Western Regions.

PRECIOUS STREAM. Oh, indeed! The royal seal of the King of the Western Regions! I must kneel down and ask Your Majesty's favor.

HSIEH. *(Returns seal to* PROPERTY MAN*)* Who is she that kneels before me?

PRECIOUS STREAM. She is Your Majesty's humble maid, Precious Stream.

HSIEH. And for what purpose have you come?

PRECIOUS STREAM. To seek Your Majesty's favor.

HSIEH. You used very harsh and impolite words to me when you addressed me on the spot not far from the cave. I will not bestow on you any favor.

PRECIOUS STREAM. Your humble maid did not know it was Your Majesty then.

HSIEH. If you had known then, you would not have used such harsh and impolite words, would you?

PRECIOUS STREAM. Had she known then, she would have used more harsh and more impolite words.

HSIEH. Indeed! That settles the matter. No favors at all.

PRECIOUS STREAM. *(Rising)* Then now she must use the most harsh and the most impolite words. Wretch that thou art! *(Shakes finger at him.)*

HSIEH. *(Covering ears with hands)* Speak no more! I am about to bestow on you some favor. Hear me!

PRECIOUS STREAM. Yes, Your Majesty. *(Kneels. PROPERTY MAN L. gives HSIEH sword.)*

HSIEH. By the order of His Majesty, the King of the Western Regions, Lady Precious Stream of the Wang family is to be crowned Her Majesty. *(He taps her on back with sword.)* Queen of the Western Regions.

PRECIOUS STREAM. *(Rising)* Thanks, Your Majesty. *(Crosses down c. to audience—sighs)* At last!

HSIEH. *(Returns sword to PROPERTY MAN; crosses to PRECIOUS STREAM)* I have been neglecting you all these eighteen years.

PRECIOUS STREAM. And I have been thinking of you all the time.

HSIEH. Aren't you glad we are at last united?

PRECIOUS STREAM. Yes, but I'm afraid it is only a dream. Please pinch me to make sure.

HSIEH. Nonsense! Can't you see the bright sun shining? You're not dreaming.

PRECIOUS STREAM. I'm not dreaming. I'm not dreaming.

HSIEH. No! *(Tries to kiss her right hand. She takes it away. Curtsey and bow.)* Let us retire! My Queen!

(MUSIC starts. They exit up L. MUSIC stops.
LIGHTS fade.)

END OF ACT THREE

(NO CURTAIN)

ACT FOUR

(Follows immediately—no pause.)

(GONG #1. Enter READER *down* L. *SPOTLIGHT on* READER.*)*

READER. Early the next morning we once more have the honor of waiting upon His Excellency, the Prime Minister Wang, at his house. It happens to be his sixtieth birthday, an occasion indeed worthy of celebration. His Excellency gives a magnificent banquet to which nearly everybody of importance is invited. He also gives a special family party in his garden with which we are very pleased to renew our acquaintance. Perhaps it is because we hate the sight of hundreds of intoxicated people drinking toasts and paying compliments to each other in loud tones that sound like quarreling that we slip out of the big banquet hall unobserved and steal into the garden seeking for tranquillity in spite of our not being members of the family. The Prime Minister is still the same old obstinate man, quite unchanged after these long years, except the color of his beard, now assuming a silver grey. He is probably bored by the numerous congratulations he has received from his many guests, and following our example, steals to the garden in search of a little peace. But unluckily he is to have some unexpected shocks very soon. *(Exit* READER *down* L.*)*

(GONG #2. LIGHTS up. Enter PROPERTY MEN *up* L. *and* R. *GONG #3. MUSIC starts. Two* AT-

86

TENDANTS *enter up* R.; *cross to down* L. *and down* R. WANG *enters up* R.; *down to* C. *MUSIC stops.*)

WANG. To be the Prime Minister is to be second to none and above all other officers. To most people my post is a very enviable one, yet as one who has had more than enough of it, I regard it as scarcely worth all the trouble it gives. (PROPERTY MAN R. *places armchair* C.) If you are unpopular you receive all the bricks— (*Up* C. *and sits*) and if you are popular, you receive endless congratulations, which is even worse. (PROPERTY MAN L. *gets table from up* L.; *puts it before* WANG.) A famous statesman is like a famous actor; everybody wants to pat him on the back, and you must have at least a dozen secretaries to pick out the letters of your real friends from the thousands of others from people you don't know. The worst of all is your birthday. Once a year you must let thousands of people congratulate you on a matter which was no doing of yours. If there is another congratulatory ceremony I shall go mad.

ATTENDANTS. *(Kneeling)* We beg to report to Your Excellency—

WANG. What?

ATTENDANTS. That the Right Honorable gentlemen of the Cabinet present their compliments to you and—

ATTENDANTS *and* WANG. *(Together)* come to congratulate you (me) on your sixtieth birthday.

WANG. To the pit of hell with them!

ATTENDANTS. *(Rising)* Yes, Your Excellency.

WANG. No, no, to the seats of honor with them, and say that I regret I can't receive them in person for I am not well—not at all well. I will thank them for their kindness—I shall have to say "their kindness"—tomorrow when we meet in court.

ATTENDANTS. Yes, Excellency.

WANG. I will kill the next one who comes.

ATTENDANTS. *(Kneeling)* We beg to report to Your Excellency—

WANG. *(Rises)* What?

ATTENDANTS. —that Lady Precious Stream has come to pay her respects to Your Excellency.

WANG. Show her in. *(Sits.)*

ATTENDANTS. Yes, Excellency. *(Cross up L. and up R.; turn R.)* Show Lady Precious Stream in, please.

PRECIOUS STREAM. *(Offstage)* I am coming. *(MUSIC starts. She enters up R.; to C. MUSIC stops.)* Eighteen years have passed since I was last at the Prime Minister's house, which is now newly painted and beautifully decorated, and quite different from what it used to be. *(Moves slightly L.; turns)* Well, here is the garden at last. (ATTENDANTS *return to places.* PROPERTY MAN L. *puts cushion for* PRECIOUS STREAM *to kneel on. Up* C.; *kneels before* WANG) The unfilial daughter, Precious Stream, presents her respects to her father.

WANG. *(Rises. Peers over table)* You—Precious Stream.

PRECIOUS STREAM. Yes, Your Excellency.

WANG. My dear Daughter.

PRECIOUS STREAM. My dear Father.

WANG. Not having seen her for eighteen years, I cannot restrain the tears from flowing from my eyes the moment that we meet. (PROPERTY MAN L. *puts chair* L. *of table for* PRECIOUS STREAM. *When* PRECIOUS STREAM *rises she hands cushion to* PROPERTY MAN L.) I wonder what has made her come to my house? Don't stand on ceremony, my child. Be seated.

PRECIOUS STREAM. *(Sits L. of* WANG*)* Thank you. How have you been lately, my Father?

WANG. I have been very well. Now, my child, what has made you come to my house?

PRECIOUS STREAM. To congratulate you on your birthday, dear Father.

WANG. Oh! Why should you remember my birthday when you have no wish to remember me?

PRECIOUS STREAM. There are things which one cannot forget even if one tries.

WANG. *(In a temper)* Yes, yes. *(Calms down)* No, no. Go to the inner chamber to see your mother.

PRECIOUS STREAM. *(Rises)* Yes, your orders will be obeyed. (PROPERTY MAN L. *removes* PRECIOUS STREAM'S *chair. She crosses down* L.C., *to audience)* My father is still annoyed with me and does not wish to speak with me. I now go to the inner chamber to see my dear mother. *(Exits up* L.)

ATTENDANTS. *(Kneeling)* We beg to report to your Excellency—

WANG. What!

ATTENDANTS. —that your two sons-in-law, the Great Dragon General and the Great Tiger General— (WANG *rises and glares at them. Whispering as they rise)* have come to congratulate you on your sixtieth birthday.

WANG. Show them in!

ATTENDANTS. Yes, Excellency. *(Cross up and call)* Show the Generals in, please.

(MUSIC starts. Enter SU *and* WEI *up* R.; *down to* C.; *bow to audience, then up* C. *to* WANG. *Bow before him. MUSIC stops.)*

SU *and* WEI. How are you, my dear father-in-law?

WANG. Much as usual, thanks— Be seated. *(He waves them to seats* R. *of him. They sit.* SU *next to him;* WEI R. *of* SU. ATTENDANTS *return to places.)* Now, my two excellent sons-in-law, don't tell me that you have come to my house to congratulate me on my birthday.

Su *and* Wei. That is exactly what we have come for.

Wang. *(Deep sigh)* My heavens! Now let us talk about something else. Do you know that we have a rare visitor here today?

Su *and* Wei. No, dear Father-in-law.

Wang. And that is the great difference between this and past years; it is an occasion worthy of celebration.

Su *and* Wei. Why?

Wang. My third daughter has come back to me at last.

Su *and* Wei. Who?

Wang. Precious Stream, my third daughter. Don't you remember her?

Su *and* Wei. Oh, yes. *(They* Both *nod to* Wang*)* Of course. *(They nod to each other.)*

Wang. She has come back to me at last.

Wei. Ah ha! Now, old Su, I feel sure that our third sister-in-law is tired of her lonely life in her cave and has come back to find a second husband. We live and we learn.

Su. We live, it is true, but learn nothing.

Wang. Attendants!

Attendants. *(Kneeling)* Yes, Excellency!

Wang. Request Madam and the three young ladies to come here.

Attendants. Yes, Excellency. *(Cross upstage and call)* Show in Madam and the three ladies.

Ladies. *(Offstage)* Yes, we are coming. *(MUSIC starts.* Madam, Silver Stream, Golden Stream *and* Precious Stream *enter up* R.*; come down stage; speak to audience, preceded by* 1st *and* 2d Maids. *MUSIC stops.)*

Madam. Lofty and majestic is our house. *(Up* c. *to* Wang. *Sits on his* L.*)*

Golden Stream. With gold and silver us heaven

endows. *(Up c. Curtseys to* WANG; *sits next to* MA-
DAM.*)*

SILVER STREAM. Handsome and noble is my
spouse.

PRECIOUS STREAM. But poor am I as a church
mouse. *(Curtseys; sits in end chair* L. MAIDS *cross
upstage and behind* MADAM.*)*

WANG. Attendants!

ATTENDANTS. *(Kneeling)* Yes, Excellency.

WANG. Serve the wine at once.

ATTENDANTS. *(Rising)* Yes, Excellency. *(MUSIC
starts.* ATTENDANTS *place wine on table.* WANG
pours out wine. MUSIC softer.)

WANG. Drink, my dear sons-in-law. (ALL *rise.)*

SU *and* WEI. Thank you, dear Father-in-law.

ALL. Here's to you, Father. *(MUSIC loud.* WANG
*shakes jug; pours out for himself only. MUSIC sof-
ter.)*

WANG. Here's to the whole family. *(He drinks.
MUSIC loud.)*

ALL. Thank you. (ALL *sit.* ATTENDANT R. *removes
tray and gives it to* PROPERTY MAN R. PROPERTY MAN
L. *moves table to up* L. *MUSIC stops.* ATTENDANTS
retire to up L. *and up* R.*)*

WANG. Now, Precious Stream—

PRECIOUS STREAM. Yes, Your Excellency. *(Stands.
Curtseys.)*

WANG. My dear Daughter.

PRECIOUS STREAM. My dear Father. *(Sits.)*

WANG. I have something to say to you, but I don't
know whether I ought to say it during this feast.

PRECIOUS STREAM. A father's advice to his daughter is welcome at any time.

WANG. As your husband died in the Western Regions years ago, I, being your father, naturally am
worried about you. I have a mind to choose, among
the younger members of my Cabinet, a suitable husband for you. As I am getting old, I wish to have a

son-in-law to live with me. What do you think of that, my child?

PRECIOUS STREAM. Oh, no, Father. Even if my husband is dead, which I have good reason to believe is not the case, I should remain a widow and be faithful to his memory.

WANG. My dear child, you know nothing about life. The old proverbs say: "To remain a widow and be faithful to your husband's memory is easily said, but difficult to carry out to the end." If you can't carry out your words loyally to the end you will become the laughing-stock of everyone.

PRECIOUS STREAM. I think the old proverb is as you say, "To remain a widow and be faithful to your husband's memory is easily said but difficult to carry out to the end." If you can't carry it out to the end, that is none of your father's business.

WANG. Silence, you little wretch! I'd rather see you damned than the laughing-stock of everyone.

MADAM. Don't mind what your father says, dear.

WANG. You old baggage! You have utterly spoiled her.

MADAM. Do as you think best, and you'll have all of my blessings.

GOLDEN STREAM. And my good wishes, too.

PRECIOUS STREAM. Thank you.

WANG. Now, my excellent Sons-in-law, will you try to say something to her for me?

SU. No, my dear Father-in-law, I don't think it would be any use.

WEI. Let me go to her, and before I have said half a dozen words, she is sure to consent to marry again. *(Rises and crosses down c. to audience)* I will give her one of my most charming smiles. *(Pulls beard away from mouth and smiles at audience)* One hundred forms of ugliness are hidden by a smile. *(Crosses to L. of* PRECIOUS STREAM*)* My dear Sister-in-law, your father's suggestion that you should marry again is a very considerate one. I would like you to think it over carefully for your own sake. *(Smiles to* Precious Stream.*)*

Precious Stream. Who is this man swaying to and fro before me?

Wei. Don't you recognize my musical voice and know that I am your brother-in-law, Wei?

Precious Stream. Have you the audacity to tell me you are Wei, the Tiger General?

Wei. Yes, your brother-in-law, the famous Tiger General.

Precious Stream. What is your business here?

Wei. Eh—eh—

Precious Stream. Have you the insolence to try to persuade me to marry again?

Wei. Well—

Precious Stream. How dare you speak of such a thing to me? The day you are under my thumb you shall pay for this.

Wei. Nonsense and stuff. *(Crosses down* c. *to audience)* Stuff and nonsense. *(Crosses back to his chair.)*

All. Well?

Wei. We-l-ll. *(Sits.)*

Silver Stream. *(Rises; crosses* R., *then back to* Precious Stream*)* Excuse me for a minute, please.

Wei. Where are you going with your mincing gait?

Silver Stream. To try and persuade my sister to remarry.

Wei. *(Fiercely)* Sit down! *(Sweetly)* Dear. *(She curtseys and sits.)*

Wang. Precious Stream seems to be very self-possessed today. It may be true that her husband, Hsieh Ping-Kuei, is still alive.

Su. Yes, I think he is. I think he is.

Golden Stream. And I think so, too.

Wang. It would be a good thing to have him dead.

Madam. No, better to have him alive.

WEI. Better to have him dead.

SILVER STREAM. Better to have him alive—dead.

SU *and* GOLDEN STREAM. No, better to have him alive.

WEI. No, better to have him dead; definitely dead. *(GONG.)*

EDICT BEARER. *(Off* R.*)* Prepare yourselves to receive the Imperial Edict from His Majesty, the Emperor of China. *(GONG. ALL rise; cross down; kneel on cushions placed in a row by* PROPERTY MEN. MAIDS *and* ATTENDANTS *in row behind. Enter* EDICT BEARER *up* R.; *crosses down* R. PROPERTY MEN *remove chairs to* L. *and* R.*)* His Imperial Majesty orders the Prime Minister Wang to welcome His Majesty, Hsieh Ping-Kuei, King of the Western Regions, to his court tomorrow, and bring Wei, the Tiger General, with him under arrest. Long live the Emperor! *(GONG. Exit* EDICT BEARER *up* R.*)*

ALL. We hear and we obey! Long live the Emperor! *(GONG. ALL rise looking at* PRECIOUS STREAM. PROPERTY MEN *collect cushions that* ALL *hold behind them.)* Hsieh Ping-Kuei? King of the Western Regions? (ATTENDANTS *cross to* WEI *and take him prisoner.)*

WANG. Good heavens! What shall I do? What shall I do? *(Exits up* L.*)*

MADAM. *(Following)* You always know what to do. *(Exits.* MAIDS *follow and exit.* SU *and* GOLDEN STREAM *follow and exit.)*

WEI. *(Looking at* PRECIOUS STREAM*)* I crave your pardon, Your Majesty. (PRECIOUS STREAM *laughs and exits.)*

WEI. *(Being escorted out up* L. *by* ATTENDANTS*)* I am a dead man! I am a dead man!

SILVER STREAM. *(Crossing down* C. *to audience)* I am indeed as good as a widow already. Very silly indeed! I don't like this act at all.

(MUSIC starts. Silver Stream *exits up* L. *MUSIC stops. LIGHTS fade. GONG #1. Enter* Reader *down* L. *SPOTLIGHT on* Reader.*)*

Reader. We have now the honor of being present at the temporary court of His Majesty the King of the Western Regions during his visit to China. It is one of the most beautiful buildings in the Chinese Kingdom, and is specially decorated to welcome its royal occupant. The onlookers have to suppose that rich silk canopies hang over their heads and soft carpets are under their feet, and that the furniture is all of ebony, though what they actually see is still the same old stage without any alteration. The patient audience is requested not to be alarmed when the author is compelled to bring in a new character at this late hour of the evening (afternoon) because without him the author himself would be forced to pay the penalty of marrying a desirable yet undesirable Western lady. The solution of this problem is in the person of His Excellency the Minister of Foreign Affairs, a man of the world who must have had many affairs in foreign countries. By this arrangement the performance will speedily come to a satisfactory conclusion which will enable our patrons to get home before eleven (five) and will prove that the Chinese play is no longer than a Western one, seldom longer than "Strange Interude" and never longer than "Back to Methusalah." *(Exit* Reader *down* L.*)*

(GONG #2. MUSIC starts and LIGHTS up. Enter Attendants *up* R., *followed by* Hsieh. Attendants *go to down* R. *and down* L., Hsieh *to down* C. *MUSIC stops.* Property Men R. *place armchair* C.*)*

Hsieh. I left here no more than a beggar and have

returned as a King. Let me sit on my throne. As I came here from the Imperial Palace all the streets were filled with people who kept on scattering flowers upon me. *(Crosses up C.; sits)* If they had only shown me even the very slightest degree of similar enthusiasm eighteen years ago when I was performing my best feats of strength in those very streets, they would have made me a much happier man. Their cheers are now to me quite distasteful. My only happiness is the company of my Queen. *(He calls)* Attendants!

ATTENDANTS. Yes, Your Majesty.

HSIEH. Request Her Majesty the Queen to come to Court.

ATTENDANTS. Yes, Your Majesty. (ATTENDANTS *cross up stage and face* R.) His Majesty requests the presence of Her Majesty, the Queen.

PRECIOUS STREAM. *(Offstage)* To hear is to obey. *(MUSIC starts. She enters up* R., *preceded by four* MAIDS, *who go* R. *and* L. *She to* C.) After wearing rags for eighteen years, I now have the joy of being arrayed in royal robes. (PROPERTY MAN L. *places chair for* PRECIOUS STREAM. *Up* C. *before* HSIEH) Your humble wife presents her respects to Your Majesty.

HSIEH. *(Standing)* Thank you. Don't stand on ceremony. Please be seated.

PRECIOUS STREAM. Thank you for your condescension. *(She sits on his* L. MAIDS *upstage* R. *and* L. *behind* C. *chair.)* May I ask how Your Majesty got on this morning at your reception at the Emperor's Court?

HSIEH. The reception was a great success. The Emperor has ordered the prisoner, Wei, to be placed at my disposal.

PRECIOUS STREAM. Splendid! What has Your Majesty done with him?

HSIEH. Nothing yet. I want you to decide for me.

PRECIOUS STREAM. Very good. Have him brought here.

HSIEH. Attendants! Order them to bring the prisoner, Wei, here at once.

ATTENDANTS. Yes, Your Majesty. (BOTH *cross upstage and face* R.) Bring the prisoner, Wei, here at once. (PROPERTY MAN R. *puts cushion* C. *near footlights for* WEI *to kneel on.*)

EXECUTIONER'S VOICE. *(Offstage)* Without delay. (WEI *enters up* R. *with handcuffs on; comes down* C.; *kneels, facing audience.* EXECUTIONER *is* R. *of him with sword.*)

WEI. When I heard that I was wanted here, I became almost senseless. The prisoner, Wei, awaits Your Majesty's pleasure.

HSIEH. Who is kneeling before me?

WEI. The prisoner, Wei.

HSIEH. Do you confess that you plotted to kill me during the Western Punitive Expedition?

WEI. I confess. I only crave your pardon, Your Majesty.

PRECIOUS STREAM. Do you confess that you have been swindling me out of what was due me in order to starve me to death?

WEI. I confess. I only crave your pardon, my dear sister—eh—Your Majesty.

PRECIOUS STREAM. How can you be pardoned? No, you will not be pardoned.

HSIEH. No, you will not be pardoned. Therefore the penalty of your crime—

PRECIOUS STREAM. Of your numerous crimes—

HSIEH. Yes, the penalty of your numerous crimes is— *(Looks at his wife, who touches her throat with her sleeve)* is death.

WEI. Oh, no! *(Bows down.)*

HSIEH. Executioner!

EXECUTIONER. Yes, Your Majesty!

HSIEH. Behead the prisoner!

EXECUTIONER. Yes, Your Majesty. (EXECUTIONER *puts his sword against* WEI's *neck and starts to swing.*)

SILVER STREAM. *(Offstage)* Please, Executioner, wait a moment. (WEI *rises; goes* L., *followed by* EXECUTIONER. SILVER STREAM *enters and comes* C. *and addresses audience)* Oh, I am so glad I have come in time. *(Curtseys)* I will ask my brother-in-law for his pardon. I have heard people say that many lives have been saved only through wives arriving in the nick of time. *(Giggles to audience.)*

WEI. *(Kneeling at* L.*)* Please don't waste your time in coquetting with the audience, but go in and ask for pardon at once. (SILVER STREAM *goes* L. *of* WEI. PROPERTY MAN L. *puts cushion* C. *for* SILVER STREAM *to kneel on.)*

SILVER STREAM. You horrid wretch, you deserve death. *(Up* C.; *kneels before* HSIEH*)* My respects to Your Majesty, my dear brother-in-law.

HSIEH. Who is kneeling before me?

SILVER STREAM. Your Majesty's sister-in-law, Silver Stream.

HSIEH. What have you come here for?

SILVER STREAM. To ask for my husband's pardon.

HSIEH. *(Looks at his wife, who signs to him not to do so)* No, you have both behaved very badly to us. I cannot pardon him.

SILVER STREAM. *(Rises)* Nothing can be done now. (PROPERTY MAN R. *removes cushion.)*

WEI. You have come in time only to see me die.

SILVER STREAM. Let me call for help. *(She goes up* L., *round stage, and exits up* R.*)*

EXECUTIONER. *(Sharpens sword on footlights)* Let me finish my job. The sooner the better. *(Starts to swing.)*

SILVER STREAM. *(Offstage)* Executioner, pray wait a minute. (SILVER STREAM *enters up* R., *pushing* WANG *in front of her)* Quick, Father. His Excellency the Prime Minister Wang is here. (WANG *enters; to down* R.)

2D ATTENDANT. *(R.)* I beg to report to Your Majesty that His Excellency the Prime Minister Wang is here.

HSIEH. *(Looks at his wife, who shakes her head)* Tell His Excellency that I can't grant him an audience at present, but if he will wait a few hours, I may give him a few seconds then.

2D ATTENDANT. Yes, Your Majesty.

SILVER STREAM. *(Down* C.*)* This is no good. I must try again. *(Goes up* L., *round back of stage, and exits* R.*)*

2D ATTENDANT. *(To* WANG*)* His Majesty regrets that he can't grant you an audience at present, and says if you will wait a few hours His Majesty may be able to give you a few seconds then.

WANG. Oh, my God! *(He faints in the arms of* PROPERTY MEN.*)*

EXECUTIONER. Now for it! *(Starts to swing sword.)*

SILVER STREAM. *(Offstage)* Executioner, do wait a second! *(Enters up* R.; *to down* R.*)* Oh, quick, it's a matter of life and death. His Honor General Su and his wife are coming.

2D ATTENDANT. I beg to report to Your Majesty that His Honor, General Su, and his wife are coming. (SU *and* GOLDEN STREAM *enter up* R.; *to* R.*)*

HSIEH. Tell His Honor, General Su, and his wife that I shall be very glad to receive them if they promise not to refer in any way to the prisoner who is to be executed.

2D ATTENDANT. Yes, Your Majesty.

SILVER STREAM. *(C.)* Heaven have mercy on me. I have been running to and fro in vain. There is still one more chance. *(Crosses upstage, round back of it—and exits up* R.*)*

2D ATTENDANT. *(To* SU*)* His Majesty says he

will be very glad to receive you if you mention nothing about the prisoner who is to be executed.

Su *and* Golden Stream. *(Cross to* Wei *and* Executioner*)* That's very hard! We have come specially on his account. *(They face* c.*)*

Executioner. I am sorry. I can't wait any longer. *(Starts to swing.)*

Silver Stream. *(Offstage)* Executioner, do wait a little. (Silver Stream *enters up* R.; *to down* R.) Quick, Mother! You are my last hope. Madam is coming. (Madam *enters up* R.; *to* R.C.)

2D Attendant. I beg to report to Your Majesty that Madam, your mother-in-law, is coming.

Hsieh. *(Rising)* All right. We must rise to welcome her. *(Bows)* My respects to you, my dear mother-in-law.

Precious Stream. *(Curtseys)* My respects, dear Mother.

Madam. Don't stand on ceremony, dear children. *(Sees* Wang*)* What are you sitting there for, my dear?

Wang. *(Who has been on floor since his faint)* I was told to wait here for a few hours before he could see me or a few seconds.

Madam. *(Laughs)* Serves you right. *(Turns* L.; *sees* Su *and* Golden Stream*)* What are you here for, my children? (Property Men *pick up* Wang.)

Su. We came to ask them to pardon Wei.

Golden Stream. But His Majesty forbade us to mention anything about the prisoner. (Property Man R. *puts chairs* R. *of* Hsieh. Property Man L. *puts two chairs* L. *of* Precious Stream.)

Madam. Oh, so that's it, is it? *(Taps forehead with fingers)* Of course we mustn't mention the prisoner to His Majesty.

Silver Stream. But you—

Madam. Foolish child! Come with me, all of you. (All *cross to in front of* Hsieh.)

HSIEH. *(Rising)* Be seated. (ALL *sit.*)

MADAM. And now let me have His Majesty's word of honor that he will not mention even the name of the prisoner, Wei.

HSIEH. I gladly give you my word.

SILVER STREAM. But you said you would not mention about my husband to His Majesty.

MADAM. Certainly. I give him my word of honor, too. *(To* HSIEH*)* Isn't that fair?

HSIEH. Oh, quite fair.

SILVER STREAM. Oh, Mother, how can you!

MADAM. Silence! Don't let me hear you speak again.

PRECIOUS STREAM. Mother, darling, you are full of understanding.

MADAM. Am I? I want you to grant me a favor, and I hope you will show me how full you are of understanding.

PRECIOUS STREAM. Of course I will. Before you say the word, your request is granted.

MADAM. That is very kind of you. *(Rises and curt-seys before* PRECIUS STREAM*)* And I must thank Your Majesty formally for your favor. (ALL *rise.*)

PRECIOUS STREAM. Please don't, Mother. (ALL *sit.*) What is it?

MADAM. I want you to pardon Wei.

PRECIOUS STREAM. But you have given your word of honor that you would never mention him.

MADAM. Yes, to His Majesty, not to Her Majesty.

HSIEH. *(Rising)* But he deserves more than death. (ALL *rise.*)

MADAM. No, remember your word and don't mention the prisoner to me, Your Majesty.

HSIEH. *(Sitting)* Well, I'm—! (ALL *sit.*)

MADAM. Since Her Majesty has granted my request—

PRECIOUS STREAM. No, I have not.

MADAM. Yes, you have. Everybody understood that

you had granted it before I told you what it was, and I thanked you formally for your favor. (ALL *nod.*)

PRECIOUS STREAM. Well, even if I promised you, I'm afraid my husband won't listen to me.

HSIEH. No, I won't.

MADAM. But you must; in this and every other kingdom all the best families are ruled by the wife. My husband here will tell you that he always listened to me and he will always have to listen to me. He will set you a good example, won't you, my dear?

WANG. Eh—ah—yes.

MADAM. And willingly?

WANG. Willingly.

PRECIOUS STREAM. Dear Mother, you are indeed a darling. As I have already promised my mother, I'm afraid you will have to fulfill my promise.

HSIEH. I said it was for you to decide.

PRECIOUS STREAM. Splendid!

ALL. Splendid!

PRECIOUS STREAM. His life may be spared.

WEI. (*Looking up*) Ah!

PRECIOUS STREAM. But he must be punished in some other way.

WEI. (*Bowing down*) Oh!

PRECIOUS STREAM. I think a few strokes on his back might meet the case.

SILVER STREAM. Yes, I, too, think that he ought to be beaten, for he has behaved very badly to me.

PRECIOUS STREAM. Yes, he really deserves to be beaten severely.

WEI. Oh, no. I'd rather die; I'd rather die! (*He grabs sword and places it at his neck.* EXECUTIONER *swings but* WEI *ducks just in time.*)

HSIEH. Attendants!

ATTENDANT. Yes, Your Majesty.

HSIEH. Release the prisoner and bring him here to be beaten.

ATTENDANT. Yes, Your Majesty.

EXECUTIONER. *(Throws sword on the ground)* Bad luck! I have been deprived of my diversion to-day. *(He exits up* L. ATTENDANTS *come forward and* WEI C. *before* HSIEH. ATTENDANT L. *takes the handcuffs and gives them to* PROPERTY MAN L. PROPERTY MAN R. *places cushions* C. *for* WEI *to kneel on.* PROPERTY MAN L. *picks up sword; takes it* L.*)*

HSIEH. *(Looks at his wife—she holds up four fingers)* Give him four hundred strokes on the back.

ATTENDANT. Yes, Your Majesty. (PROPERTY MAN L. *gives* ATTENDANT *stick.* PROPERTY MAN R. *ditto.* ATTENDANT L. *holds stick in front of* WEI'S *back.*)

WEI. I shall be a dead man long before they've finished.

HSIEH. Beat him!

PRECIOUS STREAM. Stop! Forty strokes will be enough.

HSIEH. All right, forty strokes.

ATTENDANTS. *(Together)* Yes, Your Majesty. *(Count aloud)* Five!

WEI. *(Yells)* Ouch!

ATTENDANTS. Ten!

WEI. Ouch!

ATTENDANTS. Fifteen!

WEI. Ouch!

ATTENDANTS. Twenty!

WEI. Ouch!

ATTENDANTS. Twenty-five.

WEI. Ouch!

ATTENDANTS. Thirty.

WEI. Ouch!

ATTENDANTS. Thirty-five.

WEI. Ouch!

ATTENDANTS. Forty!

WEI. Ouch!

ATTENDANTS. We have given him forty strokes, Your Majesty.

HSIEH. You may leave him here.

ATTENDANTS. Yes, Your Majesty. *(They hand sticks to* PROPERTY MEN *and retire to their places down* R. *and down* L.*)*

PRECIOUS STREAM. Now let bygones be bygones and take a seat beside your wife. (WEI *rises.)*

SILVER STREAM. You must thank their Majesties. (PROPERTY MAN R. *puts chair* R. *for* WEI.)

WEI. *(Rising)* Oh, thank you indeed! Ouch! Ouch! *(Goes to chair* R., *tries to sit, finds it impossible to do so, rises and leans over back of chair.)*

SILVER STREAM. *(Rising)* Why don't you sit down? Why do you stand in such a ridiculous position?

WEI. How can I sit down with wounds like mine?

SILVER STREAM. This will keep you from being naughty for a long time. *(Sits.)*

MADAM. Yes, it will. *(To* WANG*)* Don't be cross, dear. Aren't you delighted to see all our children happily united?

WANG. I am.

PRECIOUS STREAM. Oh, dear Mother, there is a member who has lately joined our family. You mustn't go before meeting her.

ALL. Who is she?

PRECIOUS STREAM. My sister-in-law. *(To* HSIEH*)* Isn't she your sister, dear?

HSIEH. *(Uncomfortably)* Eh—eh—yes.

MADAM. But we never heard before that you had a sister.

PRECIOUS STREAM. Neither had he until recently. I haven't even seen her yet.

GOLDEN STREAM. Where is she?

PRECIOUS STREAM. I know that she is awaiting an audience here.

SILVER STREAM. Request her to come at once, please.

PRECIOUS STREAM. Yes, please.

HSIEH. Attendants!

ATTENDANTS. Yes, Your Majesty.

HSIEH. Request the presence of Her Highness—

PRECIOUS STREAM. His sister.

HSIEH. —immediately!

ATTENDANTS. Yes, Your Majesty. (ATTENDANTS *cross upstage, turn* R. *and call*) His Majesty requests the presence of Her Highness, his sister.

PRINCESS. *(Offstage)* To hear is to obey.

(MUSIC starts. MA TA and KIANG HAI enter R.; come down R.C. and L.C. PRINCESS to C. MUSIC stops.)

MA TA. I beg to report to Your Highness that this is the Court of His Majesty.

PRINCESS. Indeed! *(She looks around.)* What a queer place it is! China is indeed a queer land. Everything is just the opposite to our country. To one who has been born and bred in the Western Regions and accustomed to the freedom there, their punctilious etiquette and strange customs are most trying. *(She turns and looks at HSIEH.)* Ma Ta and Kiang Hai!

MA TA *and* KIANG HAI. Yes, Your Highness.

PRINCESS. Who is the man sitting there like the King of Heaven?

MA TA. He is His Majesty, our King.

PRINCESS. How changed he is! I'm a little afraid of him. And who is that little goddess sitting next to His Majesty?

KIANG HAI. The famous Precious Stream of the Wang family. She is his wife.

PRINCESS. *(Starts L.)* Oh, I can't abide this. Let us go back to the Western Regions.

MA TA *and* KIANG HAI. *(Stopping her)* Oh, no, we can't.

PRINCESS. What am I to do?

MA TA. You must go to her and salute her.

PRINCESS. I won't salute her.

KIANG HAI. If you don't, they will say that the women of the Western Regions have very bad manners.

PRINCESS. Then I must do it for the reputation of our women.

MA TA *and* KIANG HAI. *(Step R. and L. three steps)* Yes, Your Highness.

PRINCESS. *(Upstage R.C.)* My respects to you, the famous Precious Stream of the Wang family. *(She gives her a military salute. PRECIOUS STREAM raises both hands. Down C.)* Ma Ta and Kiang Hai!

MA TA *and* KIANG HAI. *(Cross in three steps)* Yes, Your Highness?

PRINCESS. Why does she appear to try to fly when I salute her?

MA TA. She isn't flying; she's returning your salute.

PRINCESS. That is not a salute.

KIANG HAI. *(Saluting)* She's never done this before. Their way of saluting is quite different to ours.

PRINCESS. What is the difference?

MA TA. Our way of saluting is like raising the hand to hit a dog. *(Salutes.)*

KIANG HAI. Their mode of saluting is like churning cream. *(Churns cream.)*

PRINCESS. *(Trying to churn cream)* How ridiculous!

MA TA. They say that the hitting a dog salute is equally, if not more, ridiculous.

PRINCESS. Well, I must try to churn cream in her honor.

MA TA *and* KIANG HAI. *(Back three steps)* Yes, Your Highness.

PRINCESS. Watch me, Ma Ta and Kiang Hai. *(She goes up* R.C. *and churns invisible cream)* My respects to you!

PRECIOUS STREAM. *(Rises and curtseys)* Many thanks. Please don't stand on ceremony. *(Down* C. *to audience)* How beautiful and charming the Princess is. I now quite see why my husband didn't return to me earlier. If I were a man, I should like to stay in the Western Regions for a few years, too. As I'm a woman I hate her. I do not wish to speak to such a bewitching little minx, but if I do not, she will say that the women of China are very impolite. For the sake of preserving the reputation of the women in China I will say a few kind words to her. *(She goes up* R.C. *During this speech the* PRINCESS *has taken* PRECIOUS STREAM's *chair next to* HSIEH. *She tries to make advances to him, but he practically ignores her. She smiles at* SU, *who turns his back upon her. When* PRECIOUS STREAM *comes upstage, she rises and faces her.)* I am indebted to you for having entertained my husband for me all these eighteen years.

PRINCESS. *(Aside)* She is trying to be funny. *(To* PRECIOUS STREAM) Oh, you needn't be. I was only too delighted to do so. *(Churns cream.)*

PRECIOUS STREAM. *(Aside)* The baggage! This is my father, and this is my mother. *(They rise and the* PRINCESS *churns cream to them.)* And these are my two sisters and two brothers-in-law. (PRECIOUS STREAM *sits.* PRINCESS *moves over to* WEI.)

PRINCESS. But this man seems to have no face. *(She touches* WEI's *back. He turns.)*

WEI. Ouch! Ouch!

PRINCESS. Oh! Oh! I must go! I must go! *(She retreats* L.)

PRECIOUS STREAM. Wait a moment, please. *(Whispers to* HSIEH) So and So.

HSIEH. Oh, yes. Attendants! Request So and So
to come here immediately.

ATTENDANTS. Yes, Your Majesty. (ATTENDANTS
turn R. *and call.*) His Majesty requests the presence
of So and So.

MINISTER. *(Off* R.*)* Coming. *(MUSIC starts. He
enters up* R.; *to down* C. *MUSIC stops.)* Your most
obedient humble servant, So and So, the Minister of
Foreign Affairs. *(Turns and bows to* HSIEH*)* My
respects to Your Majesty.

HSIEH. Thank you. Don't stand on ceremony. I
want to tell you that the Princess of the Western
Regions has arrived here today and hopes you will
welcome her and see that she has everything she
wants.

MINISTER. Yes, Your Majesty. Delighted, Your
Majesty. *(He takes the* PRINCESS'S *outstretched hand
and kisses it.)* My sincere welcome and respect to
Your Highness. *(As he kisses,* ALL *turn heads
away.)*

PRINCESS. Oh, thank you.

MINISTER. *(Offering his* R. *arm)* Will Your Highness come with me?

PRINCESS. *(Taking his arm)* With pleasure!

MINISTER. Excuse us, Your Majesty. Good morning, everybody. *(They sweep round stage, then up
L.)*

PRINCESS. Goodbye, everybody. Tell me, where did
you learn your charming manners, Your Excellency?
                              (WARN Curtain.)

MINISTER. In London. (BOTH *exit up* L.)

WANG. *(Rising)* Disgraceful!

MADAM. *(Rising)* Scandalous!

SU *and* GOLDEN STREAM. *(Rising)* Disgusting!

WEI. *and* SILVER STREAM. *(Rising)* Shameful!

WANG. This is too much. I think I shall retire.
(PROPERTY MEN R. *and* L. *remove chairs.* WANG
comes down C.; *bows to audience; exits up* L. MA-

DAM *follows him, curtseys; says "Goodbye" to audience and follows him off.* SU *and* GOLDEN STREAM *come down* C., *bow and curtsey to audience.)*

SU *and* GOLDEN STREAM. Goodbye; we must go back. *(Exit up* L.*)*

WEI *and* SILVER STREAM. Goodbye. Thank you. *(Exit up* L., *followed by* TWO ATTENDANTS *and by* MAIDS.*)*

HSIEH. *(Rises)* Let us retire.

PRECIOUS STREAM. *(She rises.)* Do you always behave in the Western Regions as they two were doing? Why not give me a chance? *(She tries to take his arm.* PROPERTY MEN R. *and* L. *remove the two chairs.)*

HSIEH. For shame! *(He will not allow her to take his arm. She curtseys.)* Our affection is for each other, and not for public entertainment.

PRECIOUS STREAM. *(Imitating the* MINISTER *and* PRINCESS*)* My sincere welcome and respects to you, Your Highness. (HSIEH *commences to walk downstage, round and up* L.) Oh, thank you. *(She offers her arm.)* Will Your Highness come with me? With pleasure! *(Kisses her hand to audience; exits after* HSIEH *up* L.*)*

CURTAIN

END OF PLAY

LADY PRECIOUS STREAM

PROPERTIES

(ACTS I AND II)

RIGHT STAGE (In property box or at Property Man's station)

Prop box.
Five chairs with cushions.
Tray with wine jug and seven cups.
Snow effect.
50 taels of silver.
Embroidered ball.
6 pillows.
Broom.
Dustcloth.
Newspaper.
Clothes brush.
Precious Stream's dress (for change Act I).
Firewood.
Bag of rice.
2 horsewhips.
Horse effect.
Carriage effect.
Bundle of clothing.
Square of blue cloth.
Red sword.
Teapot.
2 teacups.
Ashtray.

Cigarettes.
Matches.
Bamboo pole.
Executioner's axe.
Handcuffs.
OFF RIGHT (Pavillion).
4 lanterns.
Carriage.
LEFT STAGE.
Property box, 5 chairs with cushions.
Teapot and 2 teacups.
Ashtray, cigarettes and matches.
Chinese book.
Snow effect.
Inkstone, brush, and paper on tray.
6 pillows.
Newspaper.
Broom.
Dustcloth.
Chopsticks and bowl.
Small stool.
Wicker basket.
OFF LEFT (Table).

(Off stage ready for Acts III and IV)

OFF RIGHT
Tray with wine pitcher and 2 cups.
Tray with large wine pitcher and large mugs.
Inkstand, quill pen, and paper.
6 spears.
The pass.
Imperial Edict.
Cloth letter.
OFF LEFT
Archer's Bow.
Green Sword.
Yellow Flag.

Royal Seal.
Bamboo pole.

PROPERTY DESCRIPTION

Prop box—black wooden box, no top, 18" wide, 30" long, 24" deep.

Chairs—Chinese chairs.

Cushions—red, flat, tufted, denim, 15" square.

Wine jug—small, china, with spout.

Snow effect—square of black silk 30", rolled around stick with paper snow inside.

50 taels of silver—block of carved wood painted silver to look like silver coins melted together.

Embroidered ball—just that, with tassel, 6" diameter.

Broom—round, rustic, with red handle.

Newspaper—modern Chinese daily paper.

Firewood—small twigs bound with cord, 15" long, 6" diameter.

Bag of rice—white canvas, size of 5lb. sugar bag.

Horsewhips—1 red, 1 blue. Tassel at end, fringe every 6".

Horse effect—cocoanut shells and marble slab.

Carriage effect—3" cymbals (2), on springs at end of red stick.

Bundle of clothing—black bag, stuffed, same size as rice bag.

Square of blue cloth—silk, 40".

Red and green swords—wood in sheath, ornamentally decorated.

Bamboo pole—5'6" long—painted gold.

Executioner's axe—wood, wide blade, silver, blue handle.

Handcuffs—wood, one piece, two large ovals joined together by small strip, gold color.

Pavilion—2 bamboo uprights, 1 cross piece from

which hangs embroidery piece about 5'6" high,
6' long bamboo painted gold.

Lanterns—wood frames, square, silk between frames,
carried at end of 18" gold stick, electrically
wired.

Small stool—red, 12" x 12".

Carriage—2 squares of silk 30", ornate embroidered
wheel in center, attached to sticks, short handles
at one end to carry with.

Inkstone—flat, soapstone, small depression in it for
mixing ink and water, 4" square. Dark color.

Table—black, wood, 24" wide, 36" long, 30" high.

The Pass—cloth, blue and white bricks, small doors
in center. 5'6" high, 5' wide. Sticks at sides of
pass and door to help keep rigid.

Imperial edict—square of yellow silk, 12" on thin
sticks like a scroll.

Cloth letter—white silk, 12" x 6", red characters on
it.

Archer's bow—ornate gold bow, no string.

Yellow flag—24" square on stick.

Royal seal—6" block, covered with red cloth, drawn
together and knotted at top.

LADY PRECIOUS STREAM

MUSIC CUES

ACT I

Record
Number

3   One cue from stage manager (used to allow late-comers in audience to be seated, after READER is finished).

1A Gong #4—WANG's entrance.
    Stop when WANG starts to speak.

2   MADAM—"I will come."
    Stop when MADAM starts to speak.

1A GENERALS—"Yes, we are coming."
    Stop when GENERALS start to speak.

2   GENERALS—"Thank you."
    Stop when GOLDEN STREAM starts to speak.

2   SILVER STREAM—"...she is coming."
    Stop when PRECIOUS STREAM starts to speak.

2   WANG—"Serve the feast here."
    (On cue from Stage Manager, fade and increase volume to avoid drowning out actors.)
    Stop when WANG starts to speak about snow.

2   PRECIOUS STREAM—"Allow me."
    Stop when PRECIOUS STREAM hands HSIEH brush.

114

3 WANG—"Let us retire."
> (On cue from Stage Manager, fade and
> increase.)
> Stop when PRECIOUS STREAM starts to
> speak.

3 MAID—"The will of God."
> Stop at exit.

1A Stage Manager—Start on cue from Stage Manager.
> Stop as WANG starts to speak.

2 ATTENDANT—"Come in, please."
> Stop as PRECIOUS STREAM starts to speak.

2 PRECIOUS STREAM—"Lead the way to the pavilion."
> Stop when PRECIOUS STREAM starts to
> speak.

2 WANG—"Woe is the day."
> Stop when ALL are seated.

3 WANG—"Let us retire."
> Stop when ALL exit.

ACT II

1A Gong #3—Entrance of SOLDIERS.
> Stop when SOLDIERS start to speak.

3 PRECIOUS STREAM—"Oh, he has gone."
> Stop as PRECIOUS STREAM exits.

2 STAGE MANAGER—Start on cue from Stage Manager.
> Stop when MADAM speaks.

3 PRECIOUS STREAM—"Oh, she has gone."
> Stop as PRECIOUS STREAM exits.

ACT III

1A Gong #3—HSIEH's entrance.
> Stop when he speaks.
> PRINCESS—"To hear is to obey."
> Stop when PRINCESS speaks.

4 HSIEH—"Serve the wine in large cups."
> Stop when PRINCESS falls on table.

1 PRINCESS—"To the first pass."
     Stop when WARDEN speaks.
1 WARDEN—"Soldiers, open the pass for him."
     Stop when WARDEN speaks to PRINCESS.
1 PRINCESS—"To the second pass."
     Stop when WARDEN speaks.
1 WARDEN—"Soldiers, open the pass for him."
     Stop when WARDEN speaks to PRINCESS.
1 PRINCESS—"To the third pass."
     Stop when OLD MU speaks.
1 OLD MU—"Open the pass for him." (Slow
     Music.)
     Stop when MA TA and KIANG HAI speak.
1 PRINCESS—"Order the troops to be encamped
     here." (Slow.)
     Stop on exit of ALL.
3 HSIEH—"Let us retire, my Queen."
     Stop as they exit.

ACT IV

1a Gong #3—WANG enters.
     Stop when WANG starts to speak.
2   PRECIOUS STREAM—"Yes, I am coming."
     Stop when PRECIOUS STREAM speaks.
1A ATTENDANTS—"Show the Generals in, please."
     Stop when GENERALS speak (upstage).
2   LADIES—"Yes, we are coming."
     Stop when MADAM speaks.
1a WANG—"Serve the wine."
       (On cues from Stage Manager, fade and
         increase.)
     Stop as WANG sits.
3   SILVER STREAM—"I don't like this act at all."
     Stop on her exit.
1a Gong #2—Cue from Stage Manager. (READER
     exit.)
     Stop when HSIEH speaks.
2   PRECIOUS STREAM—"To hear is to obey."
     Stop as she speaks.

2   PRINCESS—"To hear is to obey."
       Stop as she speaks.
1A ATTENDANTS—"...requests the presence of So
     and So."
       Stop as he speaks.

MUSIC NOTES

In the cue sheets the records have been numbered
     simply for ready reference.
All records are Victor recordings.
In general, Record 1 is used for parading to the
     various passes.
Record 1A is used for entrance of men.
Record 2 is used for entrance of women.
Record 3 for all exits.
Record 4 for the drinking scene, Act III.
Victor number and its corresponding "cue sheet"
number:

            1 — 54167B
            1A— 54010A
            2 — 54336A
            3 — 56231A
            4 — 54183B

A two-turnable amplifier, with separate fader for
     each table, and one speaker is used.
In every instance the music starts at full volume;
     and in general stops with a quick fade.
Sound effect records for this play can be secured
     from Thomas J. Valentino, 729 Seventh Avenue,
     New York, N. Y.

LADY PRECIOUS STREAM

ELECTRICAL PLOT

Front Lights:
6—500 watt Leko Lights. Gelatines #3 & 112 (together).

      1 focused L. (for READER).
      1 focused R. (for READER).
      4 flooding whole forestage.

First Pipe (immediately behind inner proscenium).
16—500 watt spots. Gelatines #3 & #112 (together).

      All focused to cover all acting areas.

Second Pipe (Immediately back of 1st pipe).
2—500 watt spots. Gelatine #14 and frost, focused on branch.
1—X-ray. Gelatine #72.
Third Pipe (Center stage).
6—500 watt spots.

      2 focused on Pavillion. Gelatines #3 and #112 (together).
      4 focused on Cherry Branch. Gelatine #29 (double).

Fourth Pipe (cyc).
12—250 watt cyc floods overhead. Gelatine #132.
At base of cyc:
4 sections—3 circuit cyc foots. Gelatines 2-#14, 1-#132.

Footlights:
4 sections—3 circuit foots. Gelatines #132, #112,
    #3.
All gelatine numbers are Rosco Gelatines. Their ap-
    proximate colors are:
            #3—Lemon-straw.
            #14—Orange.
            #29—Medium Blue.
            #72—Bastard Amber.
            #112—Medium Pink.
            #132—Medium Light Blue.

LIGHT CUES

At opening:
    All front lights out.
    1st Pipe—low reading.
    X-rays—low reading.
    Foots—out.
    Spots on branches—full up.
    All cyc lights—full up.
    Spots on pavillion—low reading.
Gong #1:
    Blue foots—full up.
    L. front spot—full up.
Gong #3:
    Everything—full up.
Cue from Stage Manager:
    1st Pipe—low reading.
Cue from Stage Manager:
    1st Pipe—full up.
Cue from Stage Manager (end of Act):
    Everything as at opening (leave blue foots full
        up).

ACT II

Gong #1:
    L. front spot—full up.

Gong #2:
 Everything—full up.
Cue from Stage Manager:
 1st Pipe—low reading.
Cue from Stage Manager:
 1st Pipe—full up.
Cue from Stage Manager (end of Act):
 Everything as at opening (leave blue foots full
  up).

ACT III

Gong #1:
 R. front spot—full up.
Gong #2:
 Everything—full up.
Cue from Stage Manager:
 1st Pipe—low reading.
Cue from Stage Manager:
 1st Pipe—full up.
Cue from Stage Manager (end of Act):
 Everything as at opening (leave blue foots full
  up).

ACT IV

Gong #1:
 L. front spot—full up.
Gong #2:
 Everything—full up.
Cue from Stage Manager:
 Everything as at opening (leave blue foots full
  up).
Gong #1:
 L. front spot—full up.
Gong #2:
 Everything—full up.
Routine for curtain calls:
 Curtain down—front lights dim out.
 Curtain up—front lights—full up.
 House Lights on—foots dim out.

LADY PRECIOUS STREAM

PUBLICITY THROUGH YOUR LOCAL PAPERS

The press can be an immense help in giving publicity to your productions. In the belief that the best reviews from the New York and other large papers are always interesting to local audiences, and in order to assist you, we are printing below several excerpts from those reviews.

To these we have also added a number of suggested press notes which may be used either as they stand or changed to suit your own ideas and submitted to the local press.

"The play is a delectable assembly of Oriental politeness, wisdom and playful satire."—*Christian Science Monitor*.

"The word in greatest abundance at the Booth is 'charming, charming, charming'. Then 'exotic', 'different' and 'refreshing'; 'novel', 'captivating' and 'enchanting'. 'Lady Precious Stream' is every one of these."—*New York World-Telegram*.

"—wrapped in the silken splendors of an Oriental prank. I found it beautiful to look at, prettily conceited—".—*New York Evening Journal*.

"All this make-believe story-telling Dr. Hsiung has related with remarkable simplicity and grace, and also with a disarming recognition of the humors that lie in it."—*New York Times*.

"—it is a rich and colorful freak, abounding in all the shy innocence and dignity that is said to characterize the mysterious people from which it springs." *New York Herald-Tribune.*

"—exquisitely dignified—a novelty stocked with charm—highly picturesque and seasoned with alternate dashes of poetry and wit."—*New York American.*

"—a precious, lovely thing—it unfolds with all the naiveté of the old Chinese conventions. A story charming, tender and amusing."—*Brooklyn Daily Eagle.*

"—charming simplicity—novelty comedy."—*New York Daily News.*

"A pretty exhibit, elaborately simple and very artfully ingenious—esoteric charm—delicate make-believe."—*New York Sun.*

" 'Lady Precious Stream' is a refreshing theatrical novelty."—*New York Daily Mirror.*

"—one of the year's most attractive and novel diversions."—*Brooklyn Times Union.*

"One cannot describe a work of such delicacy and delight any more than one can describe a rose-garden or a sunset. Mr. Hsiung has enriched English literature as surely as did Fitzgerald—this perfect play." —*National Review*, London, England.

"One of things to do is to visit 'Lady Precious Stream'."—*Lowell Thomas.*

"—this exquisite little volume."—*London* (Eng.) *Daily Mail.*

"—distinguished by the firmness of its comic outline."—*London* (Eng.) *Times.*

"Always fresh, always unexpected, yet somehow always right."—*London* (Eng.) *Listener.*

"—to give to special people on any pretext."—*London* (Eng.) *Sunday Referee.*

"Lady Precious Stream" is a play of some antiquity in the Chinese tradition. The second act has moved thousands to tears and the third and fourth have delighted millions. Now for the first time it has been translated into English by a Chinese who not only has perfect command of the English language but is himself of the Chinese stage. No attempt has been made to alter anything, so that the play remains definitely Chinese in character. Yet despite the considerable differences in the style, there is a curious resemblance between the themes and those to be found in Western dramas.

The ———— Players will present this gorgeously charming play of the Orient on ———— evening at ———— Theatre.

The beauties of Chinese costume will come to life on the evening of ———— when the ———— Players will present that beautiful play of the Orient entitled "Lady Precious Stream" at ———— Theatre. This drama, translated by Dr. S. I. Hsiung, is developed in the manner of the Chinese theatre, which means no stage settings, but the obligation of imagination terminates with the absence of scenery and stage properties when it comes to costumes, for these have been designed by Wei-Lau Fang, the celebrated Chinese actor who visited the United States several years ago.

Here all the richness of Oriental color and decoration is assembled, with fabrics of the same opulence making the stage a constantly dazzling picture. In calmer contemplation from the fashion viewpoint, one is impressed with the efficacy of the formula that has preserved the beauty of Chinese design—the utmost simplicity of cut and the play of colors through beautiful fabrics, embroideries and trimmings.

Chinese actors lead the easiest life of any actors

in the world, if you can believe "Lady Precious Stream," which the ———— Players will present at the ———— Theatre on ———— evening.

In classic Chinese drama style, the property men stay in view on stage and not only handle props, but attend to the actor's every want. Tea is served after long speeches, all faints are anticipated by cushions, and clothes are brushed after every encounter with furniture or floor. The whole performance of these non-acting actors, if such a fine point can be made, strikes the note for the complete evening.

It will be a welcome novelty to our local theatre lovers.

———

Shi I. Hsiung is an alumnus of Peiping University, and it was there that he acquired his English, there that he began the translations from the English which were to include a number of Shakespeare's plays and all of the works of Sir James Barrie. Until three years ago, when his English version of the ancient Chinese legend of "Lady Precious Stream" attracted the attention of London producers (it had achieved a 400-day run), he had never been beyond the borders of his native land.

"My grandfather," explained Shi I. Hsiung, "was a great merchant, but my father—I imagine I shall have to call him a gentleman at large—my father hated making money, and in order to be a scholar in Old China it was almost necessary that you have some sort of government post, and my father hated government officials. So he simply did with life as he pleased. A queer man," concluded Shi I. Hsiung with a beam which must have been pride.

Shi I. Hsiung said that in China the traditional theatre and the modern theatre exist side by side. "The modern theatre," he said, is concerned largely with economic, social and political questions. 'Lady Precious Stream,' however, will be done in the tra-

ditional manner. Chinese musicians will play the traditional musical instruments so inseparably a part of
such productions and the inevitable property man
will wander unconcernedly about the stage during the
action, setting up props, taking them down.

"It is not so hard to accept the presence of the
property man," said Shi I. Hsiung. "In the West you
accept the fact that there are but three walls. And
in the West it is also true that while the property
man is not seen he is assuredly heard!"

"I do not believe in this Kipling thing," he said in
what for so gentle a man was close to open scorn.
"West and East differ actually only in appearances
and in outward things. When you come to the things
of the intellect they always meet."

In order to translate "Hamlet" and other Shakes-
pearean plays into Chinese Shi I. Hsiung had to cre-
ate an original verse form. China knows no such
thing as blank verse; prose would have been a trai-
torous absurdity. The solution was a combination of
rhymed and unrhymed forms.

"The Chinese universities," he said, "are fond of
Eugene O'Neil, with 'All God's Chillun Got Wings,'
receiving the major acclaim. The young intellectuals
of today no longer devote the greater part of their
time to praise of the Soviet; the Russian influence
dwindles. Hatred of Japan, however, is everywhere.
It fills all classes. A hatred so far impotent."

"Despite this feeling against Japan," said Shi I.
Hsiung, slowly, "the government does not seem so
keen for fighting. Perhaps they know more. China
never had time to recover from the damage done by
the revolution of 1911. And still it is true that the
whole nation, even the soldiers, hate the Japanese."

In New York Shi I. Hsiung and Mrs. Hsiung have
spent most of their free time at the theatre and in
being entertained by New Yorkers—"Americans are
most hospitable." They made a voyage to Long Island

—"a very fine place for residences"—and they explored the city's Chinatown. This puzzled and interested them:—

"Something unique," Shi I. Hsiung grinned, "the cuisine— In everything it is like China and yet different, as though these were men and women from some peculiar, far-distant province of China. The dress—the dialect—unique."

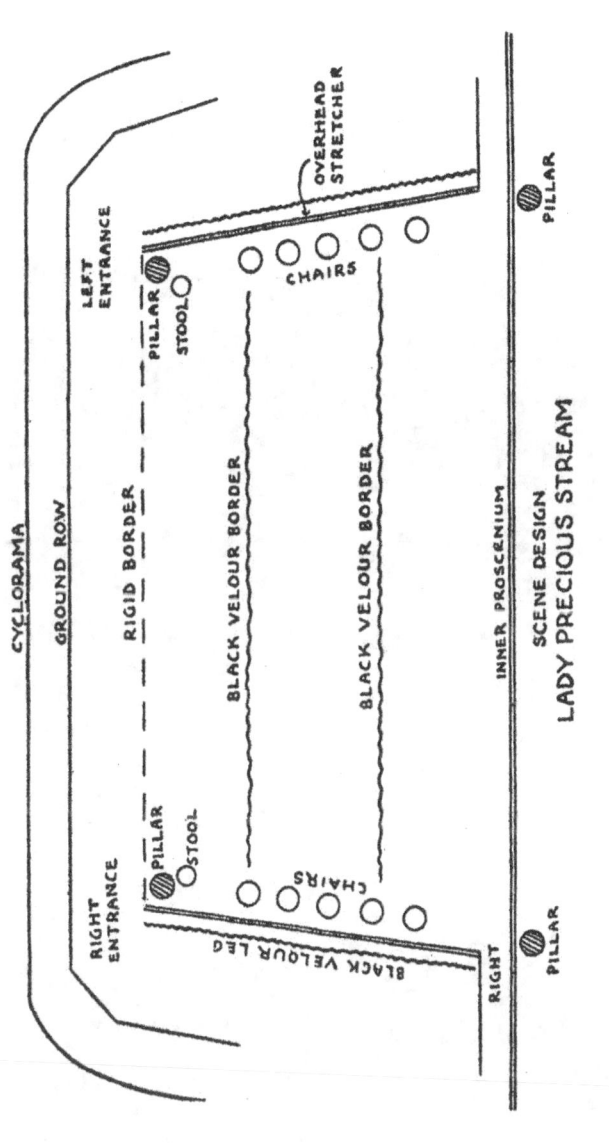

CYCLORAMA

GROUND ROW

LEFT ENTRANCE

RIGHT ENTRANCE

PILLAR

STOOL

RIGID BORDER

PILLAR

STOOL

CHAIRS

OVERHEAD STRETCHER

BLACK VELOUR BORDER

BLACK VELOUR BORDER

CHAIRS

BLACK VELOUR LEG

PILLAR

RIGHT

INNER PROSCENIUM

PILLAR

SCENE DESIGN
LADY PRECIOUS STREAM